TALES OF FAIRIES

The Tale of
DARVIN
THE Nerd

Printed in the United States of America

Cover Design by Deborah Miller

TALES OF FAIRIES

The Tale of
DARVIN
THE Nerd

By Paul Vincent Rodriguez

 Renaissance Peak

Once I was wrong when I was right
Once it felt dark when it was light
Once I was happy when I cried
Once I told the truth when I lied
Once I was surprised at how often "once" happens

Special Thanks *to:*
Caroline Dockerty
John Dockerty
Kayley Fenton
Susan Manley
Kevin Lawrence whose commitment to
excellence is partly responsible for these books.
And, as always, the fairies who trusted me with their stories.

The Tale of
The Tales of Fairies

It was late summer 2006 when I happened on a very rare occurrence. It was a fairy demotion. I watched as Qwendaline dropped her wings, bowed her head and grew from eighteen inches tall to almost six feet. She was now a human. Needless to say I was not supposed to see this but there I was among one hundred or so fairies of all types who now had to figure out what to do with me. After overcoming the shock and fear of a human wandering in on their ceremony, they accepted me as a friend.

Fairies are a very spiritual group. They believe that everything happens for a reason and that I must have a special purpose to have shown up during such a rare event. When they discovered I was a writer, they began telling me their stories.

Some told their stories reluctantly while others never seemed to stop talking. Every story was unique and carried a great message. Some of these stories helped me through difficult times in my own life. The story telling went on for months. About a year and a half after I met the fairies, I arrived at the clearing to find the entire group waiting for me. It was not another demotion. I stood nervously as the entire group fluttered up to my eye level and Qwendaline's mother, Grace, approached.

"You must go do your job now," she said softly.

"Am I no longer welcome here?" I asked.

"You are always welcome. But you have a job to do. The stories we have shared were not only for you. It is time to share them with others."

These are the Tales of Fairies as told to me by my friends in the clearing. Some stories are action packed while others are more cerebral. Some are about boys and some are about girls. I have tried to keep them short—like I said, some fairies tend to ramble—while maintaining the messages each thought important enough to share. I hope you enjoy reading the stories as much as I enjoyed hearing them.

Darvin's Defining Moment

arvin could read by the age of three. At eight, he had won the annual Creek Stick Float four times – all rather convincingly. When he was ten, he scientifically proved why fairies, like bees, should not be able to fly. This did not serve him well because he spent many of his younger years walking from fear that his theory would be proven at the most inopportune time. But it wasn't a fall from the sky that blackened his eye on his thirteenth birthday.

It was the thirteenth of October and what should have been Darvin's Golden Birthday. Like humans, a fairy's Golden Birthday is the day they turn the age of their birth date. But it was also a Friday and also the last day of the grading period for school. One last test for the semester and everyone knew who would be messing up the grading scale.

Darvin was in advanced everything. Really advanced everything. So advanced that, though he should have been in 8th grade, he was already in his third year of high school. And little did he know but the test he just aced would cripple the Touch-and-Go team and cause Cairin, the head cheerleader, to get her first "B" ever. Cairin was not happy which meant her Touch-and-Go team boyfriend was not happy and Darvin's fear of flying made him an easy target. So the shiniest thing on Darvin's Golden Birthday was his eye.

He finished the thirty-minute walk home (it takes two minutes to fly) casually tilting his head away from everyone he passed. At the base of the tree in which he lived, he stared up at the branches he successfully navigated every day to get home. He knew where each branch protruded from the trunk and kept his hands ready to grasp one should his wings suddenly fail. He felt safe flying here.

With a sudden burst, he slalomed through the maze of leaves and twigs faster than any of the fairies on the Touch-and-Go team and lit softly on the branch in front of his house. He stepped inside to the cheer of "Happy Birthday!" from his mother and father who were waiting with special fruit and gifts. Their enthusiasm turned to concern when they saw their son's face.

"Oh, dear, on your birthday?" said his mother. "I'll get something cold."

"What class was it this time?" asked his father.

"Trigonometry," said Darvin.

"Don't worry son. Some day you'll own these thugs," said his father.

"He doesn't need to 'own' anyone," argued his mother as she gently placed a cold towel over the eye.

"I just wish they would hit me in the stomach," said Darvin.

"But it knocks the wind out of you," said his mother.

"Yeah, but it doesn't leave a mark," said Darvin.

"They're just jealous of you Darvin," consoled his father.

"Why can't I just get a lesser grade once in a while?"

"There is nothing wrong with getting 100 percent," said his father.

"There is nothing wrong with getting 100 percent," echoed his mother.

"There is nothing wrong with being right," added his father. "Those of us who use math and science cannot afford to be wrong,"

Darvin was always told "perfection is something that everyone should strive for." But his was a family of technicians and engineers. "If it's not right, it's wrong," his father would say. "There is no partial credit in technology."

His parents were right. He didn't ask the Touch-and-Go team to fly slower. He didn't ask the cheerleaders to be less enthusiastic. Why should he be dumber? So he wouldn't get hit in the eye anymore, that's why. But he didn't have to be dumber to avoid getting hit. He needed to not be afraid.

So while the area around his eye turned the many shades of green and purple and blue that we call black, Darvin decided to make a change. He would not be afraid anymore. He tossed the cold towel on the table and stormed out the front door. He stuck out his chest, took a deep breath, and in front of the Gods and his parents and anyone else watching, he threw himself off the branch and dropped out of sight. His parents rushed to the edge of the porch where they heard a distant yawlp growing louder and louder. A split second later, Darvin, darted straight up before them and shot into the clear blue sky.

He was flying.

CHAPTER ONE

Shades of Gray

Black and White, or white and black if you choose to place them in that order, are two colors that really aren't colors at all. True black and true white are devoid of any hue or tint. Each has a unique and solitary purpose; white reflects light and black absorbs it. White shows everything that is not white and black hides almost everything that is not white. The colors are the ultimate rivals; they respect each other but they do not like each other. They offer no apologies and ask no forgiveness. White and black are what they are and shall never stray from their foundations. And while I believe it is important to have these types of solid foundations on which to build a house or a bridge, I think that similar hard and fast principles are not the best on which to build a life.

I didn't always believe this. Actually, it is unusual that I would even use the phrase "I think." My more common prefaces were things like "the literature states" or "the data shows." Mine was a life of facts where opinion held little to no value. That also meant that making an "emotional decision" was just plain absurd. You can imagine how shocked I was when Qwendaline was demoted. Talk about an emotional decision; I don't think any part of her brain was utilized in that one.

Now just because I gave less value to emotions didn't mean that I didn't have them. I was traumatized as much as the next fairy; maybe more given my somewhat socially retarded personality and my fear of flying.

A fairy that is afraid to fly isn't really a fairy, is it? "Look at how well that baby human walks" and "what an ugly looking cat" were some of the insults the girls would call out during my walks home from school. The boys would use me as target practice by trying to drop berries or handfuls of grass on me. Some would escalate the punishment to throwing rocks or spitting on my head if I had gotten a perfect score on another test. The meanest of the bullies would forego their flight advantage and confront me on the ground. They wanted the challenge of trying to beat me on my turf which meant they would have to catch me as I tried to run away.

Fairies are like birds – they can walk but prefer to fly. Unless they practice a lot, fairies tend to not be graceful walkers. I spent so much time on the ground I

2

could walk as well as a human and could almost outrun a cat.

No fairy could catch me by themselves so I would usually end up surrounded by three or four guys who'd take turns pushing me around until I cried. Funny how it seemed like all they really wanted was to see me cry. When I was younger, I would go straight to the crying and get everything over with, but as I got older I refused to give them the satisfaction and held my emotions in check until the event ran its course and the bully or bullies dispersed. If I held my breath, I could keep my sounds of anguish inside. The method, however, did not stop the occasional tear from dripping from the corner of my eye. I would be sure to wash my face in the creek before going home so my mother wouldn't see the water streak on my dusty cheek and get upset.

The greatest pain came from not knowing why the other kids were compelled to pick on me. Fairies who were my friends when we were younger now tossed fruit and insults at me as I trudged around the forest floor. I did nothing but be the best I could be. I used the talents the gods and nature had given me to their fullest. I was even a nice guy in my younger years. Until grade four, I was just the smart kid who walked home every day. It wasn't until girls and boys started to notice each other as something other than fairies who use different bathrooms that I was officially labeled a nerd.

I admit that there were times when I wished for a day when my fairy wing calculations would come true and the bullies would all fall from the sky as their wings faltered and gave way to their excessive weight. I imagined their flailing bodies crashing through tree leaves as their hands desperately grabbed at passing branches. For the more brutal of the bullies, I envisioned the morbid consequences of their lifeless bodies falling directly to the ground and bouncing five feet off the surface before settling in a puddle of their own blood. Now that I am older, I thank the gods and nature that day never came.

I finally acquiesced to the idea that fairies, regardless of the facts, were meant to fly. And, as you may have heard, I was pretty good at it. Conquering my fear of flying only made me more arrogant which made me even less tolerant and equally less tolerable. But it was four words, "regardless of the facts," that would weaken the black and white foundations on which I had built my childhood and turn my world very gray.

CHAPTER TWO

Losing Everything

*W*hen I was fourteen, I had it all. I was getting good grade—not as good as I had before but still maintaining my "smartest in the school" status. I had three very good friends; Gaylord, Derf and Spandlin. And, I had a very pretty girl friend who was the head cheerleader. Well, at least I thought I had it all. As it turned out, my cheerleader girlfriend was just toying with me in hopes that my grades would drop. This would bring down the grading curve for the rest of the school and allow the other students to do better than they might have other-wise. I found this out, as usual, the hard way. My friends tried to warn me all year but I wouldn't listen. Clare, my girlfriend, changed the way I dressed, taught me how to use hair styling products and had me wearing contacts instead of glasses. I was her own little Pygmalion project and, if I do say so myself, I looked pretty good.

Why was it so impossible for me to have a pretty, older, head cheerleader girlfriend? Okay, you're right, it does sound a bit crazy. What was I thinking? You know, to be honest, she wasn't actually the head cheerleader. She was just the sister of the head cheerleader but next in line to become head cheerleader. Anyway, she got to me. Pictures of her and me were splattered around my bedroom. Photos of me helping her with homework and us by the creek took up wall space reserved for maps of the world and our colony. The poster of Leonardo's man was replaced by a large photo of her and me dressed in western wear – she a bar maid and me an outlaw. She kept me going for the whole spring semester until Gaylord and Spandlin dragged me into the bathroom before math class.

"What are you doing?" I insisted.

"Saving your life, we hope," answered Spandlin.

"From what?" I asked.

"It would appear to be raging hormones," answered Gaylord. "You need to hear this."

"The reception is exceptional today," said Derf who was waiting for us with a transistor radio in the farthest bathroom stall. Derf had found a cone of silence spell in an old fairy magic book that was written before fairies had gotten so large. Nothing could be heard outside the stall once we said the magic word which Derf selected to be snarfengargle which isn't a real word and was probably why it worked so well.

"What are we listening to?" I enquired.

6

"Shhh. Just listen," said Gaylord.

Soon I heard voices I recognized. The girl was Clare and the boy was Alpho, a junior and starting forward on the Touch-and-Go team.

"Don't touch me," Clare said playfully. "Darvin or one of his nerd friends might see."

"What, you don't allow public displays of affection?" replied Alpho.

"Not here. You never know when one of them will come by," argued Clare.

"Their lockers are on the other side of the tree."

"Darvin has math across the branch next period. Just stand here and be civil."

"Can I lean against the locker?"

"Just don't get too close." There was some rustling noise and Clare's voice sounded hollow, as if she was facing into her open locker as she spoke. "My sister is such a Manx; I hate her. I can't believe she threatened to make Jenny head cheerleader next year if I didn't do this for her. I only have to keep this up one more week – just until finals are over. Then, I will be named head cheerleader and I can dump the little nerd. Are you coming to the party? You can watch me crush his little brainiac heart."

"Wouldn't miss it for the world," said Alpho.

I was amazed for a moment. I was seldom amazed for more than a moment. The others waited in silence

7

for a reaction, any reaction, but I just stood there and processed what had transpired. Most nerds are not comfortable in silence when there are others around unless everyone has their face stuck in a book. That was especially true for my friends who did not have books handy. Each began talking at the same time.

"Derf put a microphone in Wendy's locker when she wasn't looking..." said Spandlin.

"It's a senheiser 20XK15 that I found in my brother's bedroom. I adapted the radio's receiver to the wireless signal from the microphone..." started Derf.

"We were curious, you know," added Gaylord. "It just seemed strange that a cheerleader..."

Spandlin continued "...we figured it was the best place and Wendy is nice enough that we could probably get away with saying Derf accidentally dropped it..."

Derf added, "...It was surprisingly easy considering the difference in age of the two items. I mean the radio is from the 1970s and the microphone is relatively new..."

Gaylord continued, "...even if she isn't the head cheerleader. But come on, Clare?! Don't get me wrong, you are handsome and athletic and smart, even though you haven't been as smart as you could have been these past weeks...".

"Stop it you guys!" I shouted. They stopped talking as abruptly as they had started. "Just shush. I don't know how much this cone-of-silence spell can take." The next ten seconds of silence was deafening.

"We're sorry," said Gaylord.

"Yeah, about Clare, you know," added Spandlin.

"Yeah, we're sorry about Clare," said Derf. We stood in that uncomfortable silence again until Derf could no longer stand it. "I'm kind of proud of the whole microphone and transistor radio thing, though." The comment garnered a "shush" from both Gaylord and Spandlin

"We just thought you should know," said Gaylord.

While, at the time, the last thing I wanted was to know that I had been taken advantage of, it was also a very good thing that it had happened and something I probably deserved. You see, I was not a very nice "smart" person. When you've been blowing up grading scales all your life and are being told that there is nothing wrong with getting one hundred percent on every test you take, you can develop a bit of an ego. Learning has always been easy for me and I thought that fairies who didn't learn were either lazy or mentally deficient.

Either way, they were not fairies I cared to associate with or tolerate. I guess I cut the mentally deficient ones some slack because most were born that way but if you were one of those who hit the cat nip early or chose to tree bash without a helmet and took a few too many branches to the head, I had no sympathy for you.

When others would come to me with a question that had, what I thought to be, a fairly obvious answer, I would pause for a second and say, "Wait, wait, I feel a 'duh' coming on." For those who did not grasp the insult, I would provide an abrupt and sometimes unnecessarily loud "Duh!" Needless to say, people stopped asking me for help. Later, when the more aggressive nature of the boys arrived, they took their revenge in a more physical manner.

After almost three years of destroying everyone's grade point average at the high school level, Clare asked if I would go to the Firefly Dance. With an ego slightly larger than the tallest tree in our colony, I just accepted that the sister of the head cheerleader, and one of the prettiest girls in the school, would want to be with me.

She made the best out of her situation by changing me. She changed my hair. She changed my clothes. And she changed the way I looked at all the other kids. I no longer despised them but instead pitied them. I don't mean pitied in the extreme sense of the word. It was more like I felt sorry for them just enough that I actually would help some of them sometimes and I was willing to let my studies slack so I didn't get one hundred percent on every test. Explaining that to my parents was tough but I was still getting high marks so they didn't worry too much. She made me softer with every peck on the cheek and, while my getting softer may not have been the worst thing to happen to me, it was accomplished under false pretenses and that really jerked my wings.

"What now?" asked Gaylord.

"You know," I said matter-of-factly, "she has never let me kiss her on the lips. Guess I have to dump her after finals."

I flung open the door of the bathroom stall and fluttered across the large branch to my girlfriend's locker. I grinned at Alpho as I spun Clare around, pushed her closed wings against the lockers, and pressed my lips against hers slightly opening and closing my mouth like I saw in all those old movies with the great kisses I had been studying. Some of those movie kisses can go on for a long time. Mine lasted about five seconds but it was five seconds of heaven. She didn't even squirm. I think she was pleasantly surprised. Alpho was angry but what could he do? She was my girlfriend. At least for now. At least for another week.

"What was that for?" Clare asked.

"Good luck," I replied.

"Good luck for what? I don't have a test today," she said.

"We are all tested every day," I replied. I was impressed that I came up with that one on the fly. I thought it was pretty profound for my age.

Anyway, that was the beginning of the end; the end

of high school, the end of my relationship with Clare, and the end of my patience for the intellectually challenged. I was going to blow up every grading scale I could during this last week of school. It would take some cramming but I was determined to ace every-thing – especially classes with Clare's sister.

CHAPTER THREE

Devolution

*T*was a hermit the last week of school. Except for time I had to be in class, I was tucked away in my room with my face in a book. I ignored every attempt from Clare to pull me away from my studies. I ignored everyone in school and moved methodically between classes. I returned the previously replaced maps and posters to their rightful places on my walls. I replaced my contact lenses with my glasses and put my pocket protector on my shirt pocket to hold the four different color highlighters that I used to organize my thoughts. The constant running of my fingers through my hair destroyed anything the styling products had held in place.

The night before the last day of finals I allowed myself to have a good dinner with my parents. I staggered down to the kitchen in my devolved form and plopped my body onto a perch. We ate in silence until my father, not having a book to read, felt the need to speak.

"I see you are using a pocket protector again," said my father.

"Yes," I answered half-heartedly.

"You're not wearing your contacts?" asked my mother.

"My eyes were starting to hurt," I said as I continued eating.

"Interesting hairdo you've got there too," chuckled my father.

I stopped shoving food into my mouth and glared at him. "My hair hurt too," I added. "If you don't mind, I just want to get something to eat and get back to studying. I have five finals tomorrow."

"Oh, settle down. You know your father is just kidding," Mom defended.

"Why does he have to bring up stuff like pocket protectors and my hair? I'm studying," I argued.

"He was just making conversation, weren't you dear?" said Mom.

"I was just making conversation," said Dad. "You've been locked in your room all week. I don't think you've said more than 'hi' in the last three days. Is everything alright?"

"Everything is fine," I said reluctantly.

"We haven't seen Clare in awhile," said Mom, "how is she?"

"Clare is fine," I answered. "Clare will always be

fine. She's pretty and smart and will always get what she wants." My parents seemed to understand the subtext of my statement and stopped asking questions. I solemnly gathered my plate of food and fluttered up. "I think I'll eat in my room so I can keep studying," I said, then flew out of the room.

The next day I woke up early and put on the clothes I laid out the night before—on test days it is best to eliminate any unnecessary thinking so your brain can remain focused on the tasks at hand. Mom made a breakfast of oatmeal and raisins and packed a special lunch of fruit salad and walnuts for energy and awareness since I had two exams after lunch. It would be a tough day but I was ready for everything; even any distraction that might await me.

I arrived at my usual time and found Clare at my locker.

"Where have you been, Darvin," she started. "I've been calling and flying by…why won't you see me?"

I smiled at her and said, "Sorry Sweety, I've been studying for finals. I'll tell you what, why don't you meet me after school and we'll celebrate?" I closed my locker and leaned toward her, "How about a kiss for good luck?" I asked. I moved my lips toward hers. At the last moment she turned her head and my lips landed against her cheek.

"Good luck," she said. I just smiled a knowing smile and headed off to class.

The entire day was a blur. A blur is what my pencil must have looked like too as I blew through my first three finals. I never felt so confident in my life. If I didn't get one hundred percent on every exam I sure didn't miss it by very much. Gaylord, Spandlin and Derf cheered me on and brought me water between classes. We sat together at lunch and shared our testing experiences and prepped each other for the afternoon's exams. I saw Clare looking in my direction from across the lunch room but she pretended to not see me. I guessed that meant she wouldn't be seeing me after school either. She didn't, and I didn't really care.

I felt myself starting to tire. My last final, fairy history (thank nature it was just our colony's history so it only went back four hundred years) just about wasted me. I took most of the exam with my head resting on my arm. It took all I had left to not fall asleep but I made it and a burst of adrenaline raced through my body when the birds chirped the end of the day. I was free! Free from the regimen of getting up at a set time and studying and being tested. Free from having others telling me what I should and shouldn't do. Life would be summer vacation from here on out. There was only thing left on my "to do" list; I had to dump my so-called girlfriend.

CHAPTER FOUR

Preemptive Strikes

$\mathcal{M}$e and the boys were going partying. Clare's family was having a pre-graduation party at their tree. Clare planned to humiliate me in front of everyone and boast about her new head cheerleader status. Some might say I was stupid for leading my boys into the lion's den of jocks and popular kids but we had the element of surprise on our side. Not only did we know that I was going to dump Clare, but we also had been studying defensive flying techniques used by Asian fairies and were well studied in the martial arts.

"Remember," Derf said in his best broken English and Asian sensei voice, "karate for defense purposes only."

"Sensei, is it wrong to hope for the opportunity to defend oneself?" asked Spandlin.

"Heck if I know," answered Derf in his normal voice. "I know I'm ready to kick some jerk tail."

Gaylord, Spandlin and Derf came to my house for dinner and dressing. Since we were all about the same size, I let them wear some of the new clothes Clare had recommended and showed them some styling tips to make their hair even cooler. To be honest, I think Spanlin looked better in my clothes than I did. Derf got a little crazy with the hair gel and ended up looking like a super hero with his hair in the shape of a "v" which he thought was more aerodynamic.

We arrived fashionably late. The party was in full swing as we flew in a formation matching Derf's hair to the front of Clare's tree. Alpho was waiting at the door.

"What are you all doing here?" he asked.

"We were invited," I said.

"You were invited," he said to me. "But your nerd friends ain't coming in."

"Why not? You have friends here," I argued.

He leaned in closer as bullies tend to do and said smugly, "My friends are Clare's friends too. They were all invited."

"I'll tell you what," I offered, "we don't plan on staying long. I just have something to tell Clare and we'll be gone. Let us through, I'll say what I need to say, and we'll leave you to your celebration."

"You don't need to go in. She's waiting upstairs," he said. Then he hollered, "Clare!" up to the sky to which

Clare shouted an ungraceful, "What?" out the middle upstairs window.

"Your boyfriend's here," he hollered sarcastically in reply.

There was some commotion as the rest of the crowd shushed each other and gathered at the windows. I looked back at my posse who offered confident nods of support. After a minute of giggles and smirks from the crowd, Clare stuck her head out the window.

"Darvin, you made it," she said condescendingly. "Oh, and you brought your nerdy friends, too." There were some chuckles from the crowd.

"I need to talk to you," I called up.

"I need to talk to you, too," she replied.

"The guys down here won't let us in," I said.

"Yeah, they were kind of instructed to do that," she casually confirmed. "But we can talk from here if that's okay?"

"Okay. What I have to say is short so I'll go first," I interrupted. It was imperative that I spoke first. "I'm dumping you," I hollered up to the second floor. The phrase was short, sweet, and to the point. I could have used the 'we just aren't a very good fit,' or 'it's me, not you' phrases but it would have taken too long. The use of the word 'dumping' was also important so as to be as equally demeaning to her as she planned to be toward me.

There was a moment of dead silence from her and the crowd of partiers as the words sunk in. Gaylord, Spandlin, Derf and I scanned the shocked faces of the friends of the newly dumped socialite while waiting for some response that would break the most pleasantly uncomfortable silence any of us had experienced.

"What?!" she yelled in horror.

Her response was followed by murmurs and whispers which ultimately reached the ears of the soon to be head cheerleader.

"You're very pretty and I appreciate your fashion sense and style suggestions and all but you're kind of a sphynx," I added, pouring both salt and lemon on the fresh wound. Laughs began to leak from the crowd. She turned to her nearest confidants. I could hear my boys chuckling and snickering behind me as we watched Clare's social status crumble. Then someone in the crowd yelled, "Clare got dumped by a nerd!" and the chuckles and snickers turned to outright laughter.

"I did not get dumped by a nerd!" she shouted in defense. "I'm dumping him! The only reason he was even invited here tonight was to be dumped." She turned from the crowd to her nearest confidants. "I can't believe this is happening to me. I'm going to kill my sister. It was her stupid plan. Do you really think a girl like me would go out with a nerd – especially one two years younger than me?"

20

Clare's cheerleader friends created a buffer zone around her as the majority of the crowd lost interest and went back to the business of celebrating the end of school. But Alpho, and five other jocks that didn't see the humor of the situation, gathered around me, Spandlin, Gaylord and Derf on the ground.

This situation was not unique to any of us. At some point in each of our lives we were surrounded and assaulted for no other reason than that we were easy targets. We would try to talk our way out of the situation, as we were instructed, but it seldom worked. The next step was to try and fly away from the bully which, until last year, didn't work for me because of my aforementioned fear of flying. Since getting over that fear, I was able to avoid most situations as long as there were fewer than three pursuers. But my friends were not as talented at flying as I so I stayed with them. Besides, the grins on their faces implied that they may have been looking forward to this.

We moved into a four-corner formation with each of us facing outward and our wings nearly touching. I still faced the house and the crowd and the disgruntled sister of the head cheerleader.

"You do not get to dump me!" yelled Clare.

"Is that all you want; to say that you dumped me?" I asked.

"Don't cave," said Spandlin over his shoulder. "You always give in."

21

"But if I can save us from getting our tails kicked…" I answered.

"Dude, we're doing the tail kicking tonight," said Derf.

"She used you, man," added Gaylord. "She hasn't earned the right to let you down."

"What are you saying, that I can dump you?" Clare yelled.

"You can report it however you want…" I added.

"Okay, then I say 'I dumped you,'" she said gleefully.

"…but it seems pretty obvious that everyone here really knows what happened," I interjected to which the crowd again laughed.

"You just don't know when to stop, do you?" said Alpho as he moved closer.

"Hey Alpho, you and your buddies gonna beat up some defenseless nerds?" came a call from the crowd.

"I gotta look out for my girl's reputation," he called back without looking away from me.

"*Your* girl?" I feigned surprise.

"Yeah, *my* girl," he smirked.

I don't know exactly what came over me that day, if it was the laughter of the crowd or having studied the martial arts or thinking that this might be my last chance to really establish myself as something other than a weakling, but my fear disappeared and I became emboldened. A smirk came over my face as I asked,

22

"Does she let you kiss her on the lips?"

"Why do you care?" snubbed Alpho.

"I just want to know if it felt anything like this," to which I performed a perfect front, two-knuckle punch directly to his kisser. Alpho staggered backward a couple steps, before regaining his balance.

"Karate is for defense purposes only," whispered Derf.

"Consider it a pre-emptive strike," I answered while scanning my surroundings for another attacker. Alpho's friends prepared to charge us from every direction but Alpho held his arm up and yelled, "I got this."

It would be him against me.

"You can stand down," I told my friends.

"Are you sure," asked Spandlin.

"Yeah," I answered, "I need to do this alone."

"Dang it!" said a disgruntled Derf as the three flew into the branches of a neighboring aspen and watched what happened next.

Alpho was one of the fastest flyers on the Touch-and-Go team and knew how to maximize his advantage. My plan was to react to his offensive attack with a defensive maneuver that would debilitate him and allow me to show mercy without throwing another punch or hurting him. But it really didn't matter what happened next. No matter who won the fight, what was important was that I stood up to him. Having a plan and knowing that, regardless of the outcome, I would earn his respect, gave me the confidence to stand my ground and wait for his next move.

He fluttered in front of the crowd as if sizing me up. But he wasn't sizing me up. He already knew, or thought he knew, everything about me. I think what he was really doing was considering the value, if any, of attacking me. What was to be gained by beating up a nerd?

I suddenly wished I hadn't hit him first. One perfectly executed front, two-knuckle punch that staggered both his body and his ego gave him a reason to continue. Still, for a moment, it looked as if he wouldn't do anything. But then the shrill voice of his upset girlfriend shouted, "What are you waiting for?!"

Alpho gathered himself and his anger and charged toward me. I held my ground, looking calmly into his eyes as he approached. His body coiled back as he loaded up his right fist to land a haymaker. I held my ground. His left shoulder swung counter-clockwise pulling his entire body around with his right fist trailing. I slid to my left as his right fist thrust toward the area my head once occupied. I quickly grabbed his wrist with my right hand and pulled it toward me as I pressed the palm of my left hand against his elbow. If you've ever had someone press your elbow in the opposite direction it is supposed to bend, you know

24

how much this hurts. The grimace on his face confirmed it. I tried to shift my grip on his wrist while keeping pressure on his elbow but he darted up into the sky breaking my hold. I had to come up with another plan.

I hoped the previous move would subdue him and end the contest but he was smarter than I thought. I had to decide if I wanted to stay and finish this or if I would run away as I had done for the past year. Win or lose I had to see this to the end to get the respect I desired and to keep from being picked on.

I held my ground, waiting for a sign that would inform me of the direction he was coming. I looked to my friends who also had no ideas. Alpho was above the trees planning his next attack. The crowd grew restless as we all waited for his arrival. The sound of fairy wings beating frantically echoed through the trees. No one could see him in the darkness and the echoes made it impossible to identify where he was. If I left now, I might fly right into him. If I stayed, I was a sitting duck and no better off than before I got over my fear of flying. I needed to find him another way. I was obviously the focus of his attention right now. I should be able to connect with him. I needed to locate his eem.

I relaxed my mind and searched for the beam of energy that was focused on me. I found it. He was coming from the east and weaving through the cottonwood and maple trees. The larger gaps between branches allowed him to keep his speed up while creating the echoes that would hide his approach. But his eem was filled with confusion. He wasn't confused about his plan of attack – he had trained for this with the Touch-and-Go team. He was confused with why he was attacking me at all. He was thinking about Clare and wondered why a pretty girl like her would have him as a boyfriend and then wondered if he wasn't being used like she used me. He wondered what his father would do if he found out that he let a nerd beat him. His father was a big man in colony when he was in school and was known to be difficult to be around when things are not going well. Alpho thought about the number of times he or his friends had picked on me and others for no good reason and that maybe he should just let this one go instead of possibly getting even more embarrassed. But all of Alpho's confusion and doubt went away when he felt a short pain in his lips and remembered that I started this fight. He was determined to finish it. I braced for the attack.

A moment later he was charging from behind me in the cover of darkness then a moment after that he was on the ground reeling in pain with me holding his right wrist and arm bent in a position that would allow me to dislocate his shoulder with one quick jerk. His eem had given him away. This time I slid inside the punch, grabbed his wrist and twisted it outward. His entire body followed and the discomfort caused him to stop flying. I kept the pressure on all the way to the ground. Alpho lay groaning in with pain and frustration. The crowd was again surprised. They watched in silence as I negotiated a truce.

"I know this hurts, in more ways than one," I said.

"Let me up," Alpho grimaced.

"I don't want to hurt you," I said. "But I don't want to be hurt anymore either."

"Let me up you nerd!" he yelled.

I put more pressure on his already aching limb. "I will break your shoulder if I have to," I said with a cracking voice as tears formed in my eyes. I was not this person. I was not someone who wanted to break another's arm - regardless of the situation. But I knew that, if he didn't give in, I would have to hurt him or remain a wimp. "Please don't make me hurt you," I begged.

"Okay," he groaned.

"Okay what?" I confirmed.

"Okay, I won't hurt you anymore."

"Give me your word," I demanded. A fairies word is stronger than any written contract in any world.

"You have my word," he cringed.

I didn't know what to say or do. It was the greatest sense of relief I have ever felt. I sensed a similar feeling of relief from him, too, as he relaxed his body and dropped into the grass. I eased the tension in his shoulder and turned away from the crowd to wipe my eyes. He rose slowly and looked toward the window where his girlfriend said nothing but simply shook her head with disgust. He glanced once more at me with a defeated look on his face and turned to leave.

"Alpho," I said to his back. He hovered in place but did not turn around. "I'm sorry I punched you tonight."

He turned his head and spoke over his shoulder. "I'm sorry I punched you all those other times," he answered, then took a deep breath and darted into the night.

The crowd of onlookers turned away as if nothing happened. The party seemed to just pick up where it had left off. Gaylord, Spanlin, Derf and I fluttered uneventfully off into the darkness to find a place where we might better fit in. I don't know that we have found that place yet.

CHAPTER FIVE

Tooth Fairy? Really?

*G*raduation was nothing like I dreamed it would be. Our colony sorted the students by age so, even though I was valedictorian, I was forced to watch as all the other fairies' futures were determined. As is common, the crowd paid less and less attention to the graduates as more and more of them exited the Great Cottonwood with their new wings. There were very few surprises that year and the crowd was in full conversation when my name was finally called.

I looked back toward the crowd to see only my parents and my close friends watching me. Why would this be any different than the previous fourteen years of my life? I smiled at my few fans and stepped confidently into the dark hole in the tree like a man certain of what the future held.

"The answers you seek are in the colors of the moon," is what the Great Cottonwood said before ejecting me with my Tooth Fairy wings. I was not prepared for this. Neither was the rest of the colony as evidenced by the stunned hush that swept through the crowd. I expected to get another pair of temporary wings – the kind you get when you are going on to Additional Education. I never asked to be a Tooth Fairy nor did I desire to have anything to do with humans - who are definitely a lower species. I looked around me and saw a number of others going on to Add Ed, including the previous head cheerleader, and wondered why I had been stuck with the disgusting and unsanitary task of trading money for teeth.

I spent the next day wondering what had happened and how the Great Cottonwood could make such a huge mistake. There were stories of past errors made by the large tree but they were very few and usually only after it had been struck by lightning or shaken by an earthquake. That is why graduations are delayed two days after a major storm. Because there were no storms or even high winds the past week, I was bound by colony rules to report to Tooth Fairy training two days after graduation.

"I'm here for training but I don't think I'm supposed to be here," I said to the Tooth Fairy Manager as I handed him my diploma.

"If you've got Tooth Fairy wings, you're supposed to be here," he answered gruffly.

"I just think the tree made a mistake," I said.

"Haven't heard that one in about an hour," he mumbled as he shuffled through some paperwork. "Listen kid, when you've been around as long as me, you'll realize that the Great Cottonwood doesn't make mistakes. You're here for a reason." He handed me a golden leaf and directed me toward a female fairy named Columbine. "You're with her," he said.

Columbine wore a wool suit and kept her hair pulled back into a bun. I could see the frames of her eyeglasses as I approached. Everything about her appearance was neat and organized. I hoped that attitude wasn't limited to her attire.

"Miss Columbine?" I asked as I approached.

Her back remained perfectly straight as she rotated effortlessly, as if on an axis, and turned to face me. I knew I must have the right person because she had a Columbine flower pinned perfectly to her lapel. "Yes, can I help you?" she articulated.

"I guess I'm your new trainee," I answered.

"You guess?" she said curtly. "You sound uncertain of yourself. Doubt is not something I was expecting from you, Darvin."

"You know who I am?" I asked surprised.

"Well of course I know who you are," she answered. "I research each of my trainees as thoroughly as possible before I accept them."

31

"Accept them?" I wondered allowed.

"Fairies of my stature aren't required to take trainees," she divulged. "I was asked specifically to work with you. You have a bit of a superiority complex, don't you?"

"I don't tolerate idiots," I replied smugly.

"Wait, wait, I feel a 'duh' coming on?" she recited. "I must agree, that does not sound very tolerant at all." She gave me a sage look that begged for a confirming reply from me but must have been rhetorical since she just sighed, turned away, and said in a very direct manner, "Follow me."

I followed her to an area tucked back into the woods where a human window was suspended in mid air. A sign attached to the top read "Not a real window." The sign attached to the bottom read "For practice only."

"I was asked to work with you because you are a brilliant learner and I am a brilliant teacher. Given each of our qualities, they believe we can shorten your training time. We have lost a number of good people to retirement and need to restock our numbers quickly. In twenty-one years as a trainer, not one of my students has been caught, ever. It is important that you know that I do everything by the book. From what I understand, so do you."

"To be honest, I don't think I'm supposed to be

here," I interrupted. "I thought I would be studying engineering or something similar." She just stared at me. "I think the tree made a mistake," I said.

"Yes, I've heard," she answered with a look of contempt. Then she methodically continued, "Let's begin. The history of fairies trading money for teeth goes back over four thousand years when Irk, a Mischief Fairy, came upon a boy struggling to remove a difficult tooth that had been loosened when his father accidentally struck him with the back of his hand."

"Accidentally?" I doubted.

"Accidentally," she confirmed. "Sympathetic to the child's plight, Irk exchanged a coin for the tooth as the child slept. After witnessing the excitement of the child the following morning, Irk had a new personal mission and select fairies have been working nights ever since."

"Wasn't Irk mentally challenged?" I asked.

"I have provided you the official story on the topic as I am bound to do per training manual page ten, paragraph three," she noted as she moved toward the window.

"I heard he was actually more of a Collector Fairy than Mischief Fairy because he always forgot to return the items he borrowed," I continued.

"Please reference your training manual; Page ten, paragraph three," she pleasantly reminded.

"And wasn't it more of an accident?" I continued.

33

"Didn't the coin fall out of his pouch...?"

"I think we can move on now, don't you?" she said annoyed.

"From what I've heard, half the fairies called him Irk the idiot," I continued.

"I said we can move on," Columbine stated through clenched teeth. We moved on.

Columbine quickly regained her professional persona and continued the Tooth Fairy introduction. "I would like to direct your attention to the window before you. This is where we will perfect the most important part of the job: the "Drape-and-Shoot." The Drape-and-Shoot is the magical spell that enables you to get into any house or room that has fresh air inside.

Note that this window is left open a crack. Windows do not have to be open for us to enter, there only needs to be a source of fresh air into the room. Doing the Drape-and-Shoot perfectly will allow you to not only get into the bedroom and acquire the tooth, but also will allow you to exit the room with the tooth while casting only one spell. Do you see the branch on the Fir tree?" I nodded. "Watch as I demonstrate."

Using her left hand, Columbine pulled a coin from a stomachpack and held it up for me to see. She then grasped her wand in the other hand and looked around to be certain every other fairy was clear. Like she said, everything by the book. Then she drew her hands together in front of her chest and pushed them straight up toward the sky where they separated, each one making a quarter circle until her arms were extended directly out to her side. The draping action made her body turn into a million sparkling pieces of energy that maintained her original shape. She pulled the sparkling pixels that were her hands back in to her chest and shot them straight out toward the window. In the time it took to blink, the pixels flew through the screen of the window and back where she rematerialized. After taking a deep breath, she directed my attention back to the Fir tree. There, on the branch, lay the coin she had held.

"That was amazing!" I shouted.

"Yes," she said. "I will teach you to be equally amazing. Anything less than amazing and you may not get back."

"What does that mean?" I wondered.

"Anything less than a perfect transaction could result in you getting caught by a human," she answered. "Some of the same humans we help are trying to destroy the fantasy world that we represent. It is not as safe as it used to be out there."

As Columbine turned to leave, I'm sure she heard me repeat the words "drape-and-shoot" followed by a loud thud. Fortunately the window was made of plastic.

"You will need a wand to be amazing," she said as she pirouetted to see me holding my head beside the practice window. "Are you injured?"

"I'll be fine," I mumbled.

"I'm sorry, I could not hear you," she said smugly.

"I'm fine," I articulated.

"Good," she replied casually. "Let's get you a wand."

Columbine flew with great ease and precision; nothing elaborate or showy, just a consistent pace with occasional bursts when needed to clear obstacles or avoid other, less talented fairies. She must have been incredible at Touch-and-Go in her day because I was having a tough time keeping up.

We arrived back at the Fairy Manager's counter just as he asked, "Where is your student?" Columbine's answer was a graceful hand motion toward the space beside her that a moment prior was unoccupied. By the time her hand had finished its flourish, I was fluttering beside her. I was out of breath but I was there.

"Oh, right, Darvin," remembered our boss. "Still think the tree made a mistake?" he asked me.

"I'm willing to give this a try," I responded.

"He needs a temporary wand and a vest," stated Columbine. "The usual will do."

"Wait here," said the Fairy Manager as he flew away.

"Don't accept a wand made of soft woods," she said sternly to me. "Pine and Cottonwood are much too soft and will snap in a month doing this kind of work. The wand they give you is not supposed to last long but it can take time to find the perfect wand so make sure the temporary will last awhile. I prefer maple."

The Fairy Manager returned and handed me a polished stick about one leaf long.

"One maple wand," he said while rolling his eyes at Columbine who nodded her approval, "and one trainee vest size medium."

The vest was bright orange with the words "trainee" printed down the front right. There was a graphic of a human tooth on the other side. The vest had a strap that wrapped around my waist with a funny-looking clasp that looked like a lock.

"Get dressed," urged Columbine. "We will be leaving soon."

"I'm going out tonight?" I asked.

"We will gather with the others and receive our list of stops," she stated. "It is important that you stay close to me."

I did my best to keep up with my swift and agile teacher while trying to put on the vest and not lose my new, temporary wand. I arrived at the edge of a clearing in the trees where Columbine waited beside a sign that read "No Fly Zone." All the fairies, who I assumed were Tooth Fairies, were walking. I finished putting on the vest and closed the clasp.

"This is a no fly zone," stated Columbine as she touched the tip of her wand to the clasp. "It was my idea.

I borrowed it from the humans. One thing most humans do well is wait their turn. You may have seen the lines that they form at busy places in their world. While waiting in line may not be fun, it is fair and civilized and offers a semblance of order. Before this was categorized a "no fly zone," everyone just darted as quickly as they could to the manager's counter when the previous fairy left. It became a race to see who could get there first. Being that we are all very fast flyers, we had many "ties" which resulted in injuries to many different body parts but most often to the head. One time Fan's head went straight through the manager's desk. It had become more dangerous to turn in our teeth than to retrieve them from the humans. I hope you are comfortable walking."

"Walking?" I said with disdain, "You should see me run."

"I should like to learn more about your running sometime," she replied. "But now, we must get our list of stops."

We stood among the many different Tooth Fairies who had gathered from all reaches of our colony. As with any fairy job - except mischief fairies who kept their own very flexible schedules - there was one location where those specialists would meet. Tooth fairies met in the center of the colony.

My image of Tooth Fairies, I guess, as with all other groups of fairies, was that they all looked the same. They were all slender and athletic and wore tight clothes for better aerodynamics and had perfect hair and teeth and, you know, looked like Tooth Fairies. I was wrong. I was really wrong. This mess of fairies was comprised of a little bit of everything. They were tall and short and fat and skinny. They were old and young and quiet and boisterous. Some were proper and professional like Columbine and some were slovenly and casual like one that shall go nameless.

Dusk came quickly. I watched the sun drop behind the foothills and admired the north star and the moon as they took the sun's place as the dominant items in the sky. I remembered the times that Gaylord, Spandlin and I would perch atop the trees on non-school nights and watch the night workers launch. The Fairy Manager took his position behind the high desk and began belting out his daily warning.

"Your attention please," he spoke with little response from the gathered fairies. "Your attention please," he repeated civilly receiving no more respect than before. Finally he shouted, "Everyone shut up and listen!" It was instantly quiet. "Am I asking you to break a wing by showing me a little respect in front of the new recruits?" he called out. He gathered himself and began again. "I first would like to wish Jasmine and Sassy the best of luck in their retirement. Thank you for your many years of service. You were two of the finest

T.F.s to fly these skies." The gathered fairies applauded the announcement which the Fairy Manager followed with a few obligatory hand claps. "I would also like to welcome our new trainees. I hope each of you will listen carefully to your trainers and do exactly as they say. And don't get caught. Get caught and your wings fall off."

"What?!" I asked Columbine with fear and surprise.

"They grow back as soon as you get fresh air," she said casually. "Henry always makes a big deal out of getting caught."

"Sounds like a good thing to make a big deal about," I replied.

"Finally, we have a big work load tonight," Henry, the Fairy Manager, continued. "The human's Easter holiday was only a couple months ago and the chocolate and those sugar-coated marshmallow things are taking their toll. You fairies doing quarters tonight will be especially busy."

Columbine looked at me and said, "We are doing dollars tonight."

"Is that good?" I asked.

"For training? Yes. The routes are much smaller," she answered.

"We understand that you may not get to every house tonight," the Fairy Manager continued, "any teeth missed will be added to the list tomorrow night. If you are a substitute covering another fairy's route, please remind me that you will not be on that route tomorrow night when you check in your teeth. Are there any questions?"

There was some light mumbling from the crowd as the Fairy Manager scanned the group who had heard it all before. After confirming that there were no questions, the Fairy Manager scooped up two stacks of small slips of paper in his hands and raised them above his head as each fairy in the crowd raised one closed fist into the air.

"To Irk!" shouted the Fairy Manager as he opened his hands, releasing the papers.

"To Irk!" shouted the crowd of fairies as they opened their raised fists.

The stacks of paper swirled in the air as each sheet darted toward the hand of the fairy to whom they were assigned. Columbine didn't even look to see where her list was coming from and didn't close her hand around it with much immediacy.

"My first piece of advice," she said to me, "don't close your hand around the paper until it has had a chance to settle down from its flight. Paper gets very excited when given the chance to fly. Grasping it before it is quiet can result in some very nasty paper cuts."

I watched the slip of paper float and dance and ultimately lay flat against her palm. Without looking, Columbine calmly folded her fingers down over settled parchment.

"Shall we go?" she asked rhetorically. "Try to keep up," she added just before darting into the sky.

CHAPTER SIX

A Very Short Training Period

$\mathscr{B}$ecause fairies don't travel far from our homes, it didn't take long to reach our first stop of the night. We hovered high above a human neighborhood peering down on one particular house that had a green glow coming from one of the bedrooms.

"That green glow is where our tooth is," Columbine said calmly.

"So we just go down and do the Drape-and-Shoot and we're done?" I asked.

"Maybe twenty years ago," she said firmly. "Now, we must first check that there is no mischief laid out for us. We must inspect the windows and doors to confirm that there is proper ventilation. If there is no way for fresh air to get into the room, we do not enter. Without fresh air, our wings will disintegrate and fall off. Without wings there is no magic. You will be caught."

"Why do our wings disintegrate?" I asked.

"I don't know," she answered.

"But you know everything," I said sarcastically.

"Whatever gave you that idea?" she replied. "I have better things to do with my spare time than try to solve the mysteries of our world." She adjusted her suit coat and checked the flower on her lapel then said to me in a businesslike manner, "Shall we?"

We flew quickly to the window of the bedroom she would be entering. She fluttered silently outside the window pane looking carefully into the room and checking the window frame for alterations. When things looked clear, she nodded in my direction and I approached.

"This is a textbook transaction," she whispered. "You may look."

On the other side of the slightly open window was a bedroom where a young girl slept. The walls were painted pink from the floor to about twelve leaves high. Twelve leaves is similar to a yard or meter if using one of your human units of measurement. Above the pink was a white wooden border above which was painted a creamy white color that went up to and across the ceiling. There were assorted dolls and figurines neatly displayed around the room. The little girl slept peacefully under a comforter with pictures of a princess and forest animals that all looked unusually happy. Whoever drew them obviously knew very little about the difficulties of surviving in a forest. The little girl's head lay atop a small, worn quilt which covered her pillow. Everything was tinted with the same green color we had seen from above.

"The tooth is under the pillow," said Columbine. "Most times the tooth will simply be lying between the pillow and the bottom sheet or mattress. Sometimes the tooth is in a plastic case or a small wooden box. In these cases it is important to try and leave the money in these boxes. If the box is too small, leaving the money under the box is sufficient. In the event that the tooth has fallen behind the bed, the prudent thing to do is to retrieve the tooth but still leave the money under the pillow. If the child is such a restless sleeper that the money falls behind the bed, well we have at least done our job, haven't we? If the parents or child have done us the favor of leaving the tooth on a dresser or shelf, leave the money where the tooth was left. Most importantly, get the tooth. If you want to have this job for more than a week, you will be certain that your bank and your tooth count reconcile. Now, before I retrieve the tooth, do you have any questions?" she asked as she deliberately removed a human dollar bill from her satchel.

Being the inquisitive fairy that I am, I had numerous questions but opted instead to watch and learn. "No," I said.

"Very well, then," she said matter-of-factly. "Please move away from the window."

I fluttered backward as she took two great breaths of fresh air and raised her hands above her head. I heard her say the words "drape-and-shoot" and I felt a short breeze move toward the window and almost immediately another breeze move back in the opposite direction. That quickly she was back fluttering confidently in front of me. She unfolded her fingers to show me the tooth in the palm of her hand.

"Would you be a gent and hold this for me?" she asked as she rolled the tooth into my hand. "I need to fix my hair."

I stared at the amazing, stone-like piece of displaced human bone and looked back into the bedroom from which it came. The green glow was gone but the child still lay happily asleep on her quilt covered pillow. Columbine quickly fixed the four hairs that had come loose from her bun during the transaction then plucked the tooth from my hand and tucked it into her tooth bag.

"One dollar, one tooth," she said as she watched the child's name and address fade from her list and another take its place. "Shall we move on?"

Nine more stops and all pretty much the same – the only real difference was the gender of the child and the decorations in the room. I became antsy about the sixth house and decided I would go inside, too. The only thing stopping me at the practice window was a wand.

46

I held my polished maple stick close and waited for a moment when Columbine was distracted. My chance came when she stopped to count her bank.

"Oh look," I said while pretending to be interested in the child's room, "he has one of those video game players." I quickly thrust my hands and my wand into the air, recited "drape-and-shoot," and thrust myself unsuccessfully into another window pane. Columbine didn't even turn around.

"There's no tooth in there," she said calmly. "We are no longer invited to enter."

"You could have mentioned that earlier," I groaned.

"I do seem to recall asking if you had any questions," she replied smugly. She looked at her list and watched as the previous name faded away and the words "list complete" appeared. "We are done," she said. "Let's go home."

The sun rose over our colony and the human neighborhood that surrounded us. The same group of fairies that had gathered a few hours before now stood silent, fatigued and disheveled in the line that Columbine had so proudly recommended. There was no magic to turning in your teeth at the end of the night. Each fairy took a turn with the Fairy Manager who counted the teeth and checked their bank. It was a long and arduous process that I felt didn't concern me since I had neither teeth to turn in nor human money to return. Besides, there was something I wanted to see for myself.

Columbine permitted me to leave and reminded me to be back at dusk to continue my training. She touched the clasp on the trainee vest with her wand popping it open and allowing me to remove the uncomfortable piece of attire which I left with her. I darted through the light morning fog to the window of the first child we had visited. I hovered outside her window as the sun rose over the neighboring rooftops and a beam of light shot through the glass. I watched as her little eyes squinted to keep the light out, then, realizing defeat, blinked, quickly at first and then slower and slower until they no longer closed. Nothing on her body moved except her small fingers that played with the yarn knots used to tie the quilted top of her blanket to the batting below. She looked as if she had been awakened for the first time. Her mind had no agenda. She had no thoughts from the previous day that needed addressing. She had no "To Do" list with items to be checked off. She had nothing but a day of new experiences ahead of her and, as she found when she slid her hand under her pillow, a new one-dollar-bill.

I can only assume that it was a scream of joy I heard that was followed by her yelling, "The Tooth Fairy came! The Tooth Fairy came!" Then she ran to the window, and with a smile devoid of one of her top front teeth, said, "Thank you Tooth Fairy." Then she ran out the door of her bedroom to show her dollar to the rest of her family.

I was overcome by a great sense of joy and satisfaction that I had not felt before. Maybe Irk wasn't mentally challenged after all.

CHAPTER SEVEN

Patience, Young Househopper

*C*met Gaylord, Derf and Spandlin at the creek later that morning for a snack before they went back to school and I went to bed for the day. I told them about the Drape-and-Shoot and what human bedrooms look like and how excited the little girl was. I was tired and I know I didn't share as much as I could have but they were still happy to hear about my first night.

Sleeping during the day was a challenge. Dad suggested I sleep in the den which was the only room without a window. My parents off to work, my slumber was hindered only by the sounds of the daily happenings that seeped through the walls but my level of exhaustion wouldn't allow even that to bother me much.

I reported back to the clearing a few minutes before dusk and went straight to the practice window. I gripped my wand in my left hand and took two deep breaths to clear my head so I could focus on my destination and my path. "Drape and shoot," I recited as I performed the arm and hand motions precisely. My body dematerialized into energy particles that shot through the open window and rematerialized on the other side. I paused before assessing my physical condition. I hesitantly grasped my left forearm with my right hand. After confirming that it was again solid, I checked my head and my torso which I also confirmed still had clothing. Doing a proper Drape-and-Shoot, but ending up naked, would have presented a unique level of disappointment. I shot my wand up into the air and shouted, "Yes!" Then, I am embarrassed to say, I started dancing while singing some made-up lyrics that proclaimed my greatness. Fortunately my elation was interrupted before I got too crazy.

"The trick is getting back," said Columbine from the other side of the window. She was, of course, impeccably dressed - her hair again in a bun. The lapel of her blue wool suit adorned with a fresh, blue Columbine flower. "You slept I hope," she said, as I flew under the practice window to greet her.

"Some," I stated.

"You will adjust," she said. "Come, we have a busy night ahead I am told."

We joined the others waiting to receive their lists of stops for the night. "How do you get back?" I asked While the fairy manager made his nightly announcements.

"The same way you get in," she said.

"The Drape-and-Shoot?" I confirmed.

"Yes," she said.

"But how do you do it so quickly?" I asked. "It's as if you never rematerialize when you go in."

"I have a lot of experience," she said.

"Will I be in training until I can do it like you?" I asked.

"I don't think the colony can wait that long," she said. "Don't think that means you can take this training lightly."

"But if ninety-nine percent of my assignments will be like last night…" I argued.

"Ninety-nine is not one-hundred," she said as the Fairy Manager entered the clearing. "It is that one house - that one precocious child or curious teenager or vindictive adult - that you don't expect, that will change your life forever," she said sternly.

"…and don't get caught," boomed the voice of the Fairy Manager.

"There's a reason he says that every night," Columbine added as she raised her hand with the others to receive her list. "Be patient. Learn as much as you can as quickly and as thoroughly as you can. Your time will come soon enough," she said as she gently closed her hand around the slip of wiggling paper. "Shall we?" she asked. I nodded an affirmation and we both darted into the night.

CHAPTER EIGHT

Flying Solo

*C*olumbine was right, my time came very soon. After one week of training she performed the ceremonial removal of the trainee vest. The Fairy Manager announced my successful completion of training with a very personal "Darvin, don't get caught" before handing me a tooth bag and a pouch with quarters in it. That night, I raised my hand alongside the other Tooth Fairies and felt my first list tickle my palm until I wrapped my fingers around it and pulled it from the air.

The list contained five names, first names only, age, and gender. All five stops were revealed initially to show the extent of my work load for the evening. Soon after I scanned the list, the bottom four names vanished leaving me to focus on the name at the top.

The names on my list glowed red. Red is the color designated for those who would receive quarters. Green is for dollars, blue is for five-dollar bills and gold is for denominations above five dollars. Purple used to be for dimes but that denomination hasn't been used for many years. Orange is for food items - typically fruit or candy, and yellow is for non-monetary and non-food items like toys. I felt these items were in conflict with other holidays and birthdays but it was explained that as long as we were trading these items for teeth, we were operating within the confines of our agreements with other mystical beings.

I wasted no time and darted up into the sky to scan the houses for the one that glowed red just for me. Due north, about a mile away, I saw it. I darted toward the glow and pulled up beside the window of the small house. Inside the small bedroom slept two little boys in a one-human bed pushed into a corner. The one with the red glow under his pillow slept closest to the wall. The other smaller, boy was splayed out across the top of the blankets and partially over the target. This was going to be tricky.

I checked the frame of the window for any foreign objects and possible traps and sniffed the air for the smell of malfeasance. Noting an absence of both, I grasped a quarter with my right hand and my wand with my left and performed a perfect Drape-and-Shoot. Now inside, I just needed to get the tooth. I fluttered above the two boys searching for a way to maneuver between them without waking either. The smaller boy, sleeping on the outside, mumbled something incoherent, scratched his nose and dropped his arm across his body.

That only freed things up a little but it gave me an idea. I fluttered down to his hand that hung off the bed and flapped my wings quickly but gently against it. This very dangerous maneuver is called the Tickle Itch which is described on page forty-seven, paragraph eleven of the Tooth Fairy manual, under the heading "Last Resorts." It is designed to get the victim to bring the other hand over to scratch the itchy target hand. This is a dangerous move for fairies who are not quick or aware enough to get out of the way when the other hand comes flying in. Many a fairy has been slapped and crushed under the weight of a human hand on its mission to scratch an itch.

I artfully dodged the human's hand as it approached quickly and erratically. The momentum of the arm rolled the small boy's body away from the pillow. Unfortunately, the body continued to roll and fell off the bed with a loud thud. I darted to the pillow, quickly found the tooth, made the switch, performed another perfect Drape-and-Shoot, and was outside the window again before the word "ouch" exited the small boy's mouth. I flew straight up into the sky for three seconds before stopping and looking back toward the house I had just left. I pulled my list from my pocket and watched as the first name faded away along with the red glow in the house. A new red glow appeared in the corner of my eye. I looked to my left to see my next assignment. Julie, age six, female glowed on my list.

"I hope she has her own bed," I said.

CHAPTER NINE

Making a Name

*O*ver the next few weeks I established myself as one of the premier Tooth Fairies in the colony. I learned how to get into and out of houses with only one Drape-and-Shoot spell, shortening my transaction time for a standard home to less than two seconds. I was efficient and reliable and always completed my list. Even the Fairy Manager held me up as a shining example of what a Tooth Fairy should be. Sleeping during the day became comfortable even though it meant not seeing my friends or parents as much.

In the summer, when the nights were shorter, I would see my parents at dinner time. I would share stories from the previous night and they would remind me to be cautious while I was amongst humans. The redundancy of their warning ultimately rendered it ineffective as my standard response of "I will" no longer had meaning either. It would only be a

57

couple months before the penalty for my complacency would be revealed.

It was October and I could see the breath of the Fairy Manager as he distributed our lists and repeated his nightly warning. The previous quota for experienced fairies was six teeth a night but I had raised the bar and most of us were now bringing in ten to fifteen. We were actually gaining on our back-orders and most children were getting their money the same night they lost their teeth. My list of red names had grown to twenty. Rumor had it that if I completed tonight's list I would be promoted to green. I would have achieved that goal a full year faster than the current record holder. I wanted that record!

The evening was going smoothly. I had a couple of teeth that had fallen behind the bed and were tucked into pillow cases. I had to loosen one from a boy's hand but that just required tickling his nose. I had some extra time so I did it again just to watch him slap himself in the face a second time. I had become overconfident.

I watched the nineteenth name fade from the list and searched for the final red house of the night. I was tired and the sun was creeping over the horizon. One more tooth and I was moving up to dollars. The red glow appeared in the distance in a less-affluent community. I was happy that my last quarter would go to someone who might appreciate it a little more.

I jetted toward the building in the distance and pulled up beside the slightly-ajar window. The room was different than the others. The bed was a mattress and box spring stacked on the floor. The boy was curled up into a ball and covered by two thin blankets and sheet. Along one wall were shelves made from board planks set across cinder blocks. On top of the shelves were small stacks of neatly folded clothes. In the corner was a folding table that served as a desk with a metal folding chair in front of it. On top of the table sat what looked to be a television set but much thinner.

It didn't matter what the home or the room looked like, I had a job to do. I quickly looked for strings or ropes that might be used to shut the window or drop a net. The coast was clear I took a deep breath and, holding a shiny quarter in my right hand, turned myself into sparkles of energy and dust and shot myself toward the window opening. The particles that were me suddenly had an unusual red glow to them as they streamed into the room. I had not seen this before and the distraction caused me to fully materialize as soon as I passed through the screen. As I floated in the air, my attention was drawn to a mirror attached to the wall and a red beam of light that reflected back to a black box on the opposite wall. A green light on the black box changed to red triggering another box above the window to do the same. That was followed by a loud pop as a metal pole attached to the top of the window was thrust downward. The window slammed shut.

For a moment I hovered above the floor wondering what had just happened. A moment later my wings disintegrated and their pieces, as well as the rest of my body, dropped out of the air to the floor. I was caught.

CHAPTER TEN

Caught

$\mathcal{I}$ landed on my butt in a pile of dirty clothes and rushed to get to my feet. I focused my attention on the window and said, "oppen winden" then thrust my wand in its direction. No magic came from my length of polished maple. But how could this be? No house is totally void of fresh air.

The sound of the slamming window woke the human. He jumped, fully clothed, from the bed and shined a flashlight in the direction of the noise.

"Ha, I got you Booker," he shouted.

The human's head was unusually large for a child of tooth shedding years. The body was equally large. I stayed as still as possible in hopes that Booker, whoever that was, would appear somewhere and re-open the window. No one came. I watched as the human methodically checked the red beam that crossed the window opening, then the triggers on the switches and finally the rod atop the window pane. The next natural progression would be to open the window and confirm that it, too, was working correctly. But the human didn't do that. Instead he turned around, briskly rubbed his arms to warm himself and headed back to bed. Just as his head landed on the pillow that glowed red marking the location of the tooth I had come to retrieve, a beam of sunlight burst through the window and bounced off my head. The human's eyes opened again and he looked directly at me.

For a moment we just stared at each other; him processing what was before him and me hoping he doesn't freak out, as humans say.

"Who are you?" he asked rather calmly.

"I am your great uncle from Peoria," I stated confidently as per Tooth Fairy rule forty-five, paragraph two, option one. "Now open that window," I demanded.

Then he really woke up, and being awake, he knew that the likelihood of an eighteen-inch tall anything being his uncle from Peoria was very slim. And then he freaked out. He again jumped out of his bed but this time he ran toward the door.

"I don't have no uncle in Peoria," he yelled.

The door was jammed with some type of insulation and a towel that had been pressed into the gap at the bottom to keep cold air out. He was trapped too.

"Crap!" he shouted as he gave up on the door. "What are you anyway?"

The recommended response to that question per the Tooth Fairy manual is to repeat, "I am your great uncle from Peoria" and a bunch of other stuff that I knew wasn't going to work. So I just told him the truth.

"I'm a Tooth Fairy," I stated calmly. "I came to get the tooth you lost."

"I didn't lose no tooth," he argued.

He reached for a pair of pants from the pile of clothes beside me and began slapping them down on the floor in my direction. "Hey! Hey! calm down," I hollered as I successfully dodged the approaching denim. The pants slapped the floor beside me once more.

"You've got a tooth under your pillow," I shouted. "Check for yourself."

"I ain't taking my eyes off you," he said sharply. The next slap of the pants clipped my shoulder. This kid was crazy. I needed to find a safe place to hide. One quick glance around the room proved that I had maneuvered myself away from all the best places. The desk was too far away. There was no bed frame to climb under and the only chair in the place was by the desk. Behind me was a big plastic box with a wire door. At the next slap of the pants I jumped into the box and backed myself to the other end. The boy rushed to the front of the box, pushed the door shut and latched it. I felt behind me to for another opening or way out. There was none. I was in a cage. I was a caged fairy.

A "caged" fairy is different than a "caught" fairy. Caught fairies are just in places where there is no fresh air. They can leave when a window or door is opened and their wings grow back. Caged fairies are caught even after their wings return. A cage is a cage regardless of whom or what is in it. Columbine hadn't mentioned that there might be cages out here.

The boy panted as he stumbled backward and collapsed into the chair at his makeshift desk. He reached behind him on the desk for a plastic looking tube that he stuck into his mouth. There was a spraying sound as he pressed on something inside it. He quickly breathed in whatever was sprayed into his mouth then placed the tube back on the desk and tried to relax as his breathing slowed. He stared at me in the cage while he waited for things to go back to normal. There was a knock on the door and a large voice called in, "Joseph?"

"Yeah," Joseph called back.

"You okay in there?" asked the voice.

"I'm good, Dad," Joseph replied.

"You talking to someone?" his dad asked.

Joseph thought for a second, "No, I was just working on the computer."

"Well hurry up. Your mom's makin' eggs," he added before walking away.

Joseph's face cycled through a dozen or so expressions all conveying a type of confusion or frustration. The more he looked at me and tried to analyze the situation, the clearer it became that my life was about to change. I stood with my arms crossed and waited for him to say something. I desperately hoped it was somewhat intelligent.

"You don't have no wings," he finally said.

"They fell off when the window slammed shut," I countered. "And I think the correct verbiage is 'ain't got no wings,' you moron."

"Oh, you're gonna mock me now? Is that it?" he challenged.

I just grinned, held my hand out to signal stop, and said mockingly, "Wait, wait, I feel a 'duh' coming on." I mean really, how could I resist?

"A 'duh'?! You feel a 'duh' coming on?!" he repeated. "If you're so smart, why are you stuck in a cage?"

"Let me see; get hit by a pair of pants from a crazy human kid or jump into a plastic box," I contemplated aloud. "Dude, I'm like the size of half your leg. What would you do?"

"You still don't have no...*any* wings," he said. "Aren't fairies supposed to have wings?"

"Open the window and I will," I said.

"It's stuck," he said. "I have to reset all the switches."

"How long will that take," I asked.

"Longer than I got right now," he answered. "I'll have to do it after school. Besides, it's too dangerous to leave a window open around here."

"How is it that you don't have any other fresh air in here?" I asked. "Your furnace should blow fresh air around the house."

"Our furnace blows air alright, it's just freezing," he answered. "The heating element is broken. I keep the vent taped closed and I weather stripped the door so I don't loose my body heat."

"If it's so cold, why were you sleeping with the window open?" I asked.

"I was trying to catch my neighbor Booker stealing my laptop," he answered.

"What's a laptop?" I asked.

"You don't know what a laptop is? And you're calling me a moron?" My scowl was all it took to remind him that I wasn't of his world. "It's a computer," he said as he slid his chair out of my line-of-sight and motioned to the shiny box on the desk.

"What does it do?"

"Everything, just about," he said. "The school got it for me to help with my homework. My mom and dad can't afford nothin' like this. Booker would just sell it for drug money."

"What are you going to do with the tooth under your pillow?" I asked.

"I told you I didn't lose a tooth," he said. He sat up in the chair and looked toward the pillow. "I bet it's Andrew's."

"What's an Andrew?" I asked.

"My little brother," he answered. "He just lost a tooth." He went to the bed and violently ran his hand under his pillow knocking the tooth onto the floor. "I don't feel anything," he said.

There were two sudden and brief knocks on the door before the doorknob turned and his dad tried to push his way through. Joseph jumped from the bed and pulled the towel from under the door. I backed myself away from the front of the cage as the door pushed open and an adult-sized human entered. He was even bigger than Joseph. The fresh air triggered the regrowth of my wings which was accompanied by an orangish glow that lasted about five seconds. The glow in the box drew the attention of both Joseph and his dad.

"What's in there?" asked his dad.

"Nothing," said Joseph nervously. "Why?"

His dad looked again at the cage that no longer glowed, then back at Joseph. "Must have been the sun in my eyes," he said. "You sleep in your clothes again?"

Joseph didn't reply to the rhetorical question. "I'm gettin' parts to fix that furnace today. With a little help we'll have it workin' tonight so you can take some of this stuff off the door." His dad stepped back through the bedroom doorway. "You better get out here and get some breakfast before school. And change those clothes. There's no law that says every smart person has to look like Einstein. That reminds me, get a haircut."

Joseph closed the door behind his dad and began removing his clothes. I made my way to the front of the cage with my newly grown wings and cleared my throat. Joseph looked over as he pulled a sweater over his head.

"You have wings," he added.

"I'm a fairy," I replied. "Now will you please open the cage door so I can leave?"

Joseph paused in the middle of putting on a clean pair of pants. Only his right leg was clothed; apparently humans put their pants on one leg at a time. He grinned.

"Not now," he said.

"Not now?" I asked. "Why?"

"I'm not gonna hurt you," he said. "I just want to learn a little more. How many people ever catch a Tooth Fairy?"

"How long do you plan on keeping me?" I asked.

"I don't know. Look, I gotta go to school. Just relax, we can talk later."

"What do I do until then?" I asked.

He looked around the room and grabbed a small plastic box from his desk. He reached for the door on the cage but stopped just before unlatching it. "If I unlatch this, you're gone aren't you?" he asked. He moved his hand around to the side of the cage and slid the small box through a slot in the plastic. The box fell to the bottom of the cage with a thud.

"I'll be back in about eight hours," he said.

"Eight hours?!"

The bedroom door closed hard behind him as the beam of sunlight turned to a general glow that illuminated the entire room. It was daytime and the other fairies would be returning to the clearing. I wondered what would happen when they realized I was not there.

CHAPTER ELEVEN

House Rules

"Seven of diamond, jack of spade, seven of clover, four of heart, king of spade," I narrated. "Keep the jack and king and draw three…nothing. Deal. Five of clover, six of heart, seven of spade, nine of diamond, queen of heart. Hmmm. Dump the queen and hope for a big payout with an eight for a straight? Don't be stupid. Keep the queen. Draw four…a pair of queens." I watched as five credits were added to my score.

The plastic box Joseph gave me was a Jacks-or-better poker game. I guess the game was usually played with cards but this one ran on a small battery. Players start the game with one hundred credits and wager five credits on each hand played. You are given five cards and the choice of which of those five to keep or replace with others. Any hand with less than two jacks after the two rounds was a loser and your five credits were lost. Hands with two jacks or better paid credits back. One pair of jacks, queens, kings or aces returned your five credits. Three of a kind paid double and the payoffs increased based on the difficulty of the combination. Ace, king, queen, jack, ten of the same symbol was the best possible result and paid handsomely. As the day wore on, I determined that the payoffs didn't really matter. Regardless of how many credits you amassed, you were destined to lose all of your earnings and your original one hundred starting credits if you continued to play by the device's rules which it listed as "House Rules" on the back.

Having lost the remainder of my credits shortly after winning with the two queens, I declined the game's invitation to play again and sat down in the cage. A square shaped thing on the wall showed the number three with a flashing colon followed by a one and a five. I heard the sound of a door opening and closing followed by the sound of heavy, trudging footsteps and the slamming of cupboard doors. There was a ripping sound followed by crunching sounds shortly after. Lethargic steps got louder and louder as the culprit came closer. The doorknob turned and there were two loud thuds as Joseph staggered, shoulder first, into the room. Words on the side of the large bag he carried read "potato chips." He munched these things as he dropped his backpack onto the floor beside the table and collapsed onto his bed.

He looked tired and mentally worn. Any excitement in his eyes had been replaced with focus, concern and contemplation. I remembered that focus and determination; the kind that came with the responsibility of high expectations and limited resources; the kind that takes you to that small place in your mind where nothing exists except you, time and your responsibilities. In there, it is easy to become oblivious to your surroundings.

"Did you bring me any food?" I asked curtly.

The directness of the statement shook Joseph from his daze. His head and eyes rolled toward me. He glared at me for a few seconds before he rolled the rest of his body off the bed and crawled to the front of the cage where he dropped a handful of potato chips on the floor outside the cage door.

"What is this?" I inquired.

"Potato chips," he answered as he flopped back onto his bed.

"Can you be a little more specific?" I requested.

"They're thin slices of potato boiled in oil and salted," he said.

I carefully inspected one of the oily items that I gingerly pinched between my thumb and finger. I had seen potatoes before, even potato slices, but nothing like this. This "chip," as he described it, was golden brown and curly and secreted a substance that coated my skin and did not evaporate like the water I had come to expect from a typical slice of potato. I assumed this was oil because, scientifically speaking, it made sense that an item dipped or boiled in a substance would continue to secrete that substance until it evaporated or dried. The oil also served as an adhesive that helped a granular substance stick to the surface of each chip. This must be the salt. This combination of starch and oil and salt could not possibly be good for me.

"Do you have any fruit?" I asked.

"Why?" he replied.

"Because I don't think my body will react well to something boiled in oil," I answered. "I'm not so sure salt is good for me either."

"Geez, why can't anything be easy?" he groaned as he dragged himself from his bed and stormed out of the room. I heard more cupboard doors slam followed by the sharp sound of metal hitting a board. There was more stomping feet as he made his way back to the room. He stormed in and tossed half a banana onto the floor in front of the cage.

"Are you serious?" I shouted.

"You said fruit," he shouted back. "What, you don't like bananas?"

"How am I supposed to get it?"

"You're a fairy, you have your wings back, figure something out," he replied.

"I'm in a cage, you jerk," I answered.

"Yeah, well whose fault is that?" he asked.

"It's yours, you imbecile," I argued. "You set the trap on the window!"

"Yeah, well you tripped it!" he said.

"I was doing my job!"

"I didn't ask you to come in here!" he argued.

"You had a tooth under your pillow!" I harped. "That's like begging me to come in!"

"You didn't have to come in!"

"It's my job!" I shouted.

"Geez!" he exclaimed as he slammed his hands down on the mattress and violently pushed himself up. "Do I have to do everything for everyone?" He dropped to his knees, peeled the banana and smashed it through the wire grid on the door with his hand. The chunks of the soft fruit that did not stick to the wires plopped on the floor of the cage. I quickly picked and ate the pieces from the door as Joseph stormed out of the room. I heard sounds of running water and assumed he was washing his hands. Bananas were a rare treat in the colony and half of one would hold me over for a day or maybe two. Joseph stormed back into the room and plopped into his chair at the folding table. He folded open the silvery box on the table and pushed a button.

"When's the last time you washed this cage?" I asked as I surveyed the pieces of banana on the floor.

"Yesterday, after I found it by the dumpster," he said snidely. The coincidence was not lost on me.

"If you don't want me here, open this door and I'll be gone before you can blink," I said with my mouth full of banana. Joseph leaned forward in his chair with his head in his hands while the display on the box changed colors and designs. "Don't think this is my first choice for places to spend the day, or night for that matter," I continued.

"You got your food," he said. "Just leave me alone."

"Who dipped your head in the pond?" I muttered.

"What's that supposed to mean?" he asked.

"It's an expression," I griped. "We use it when someone's being a drag."

"You wouldn't understand," Joseph replied.

"Yeah, probably not," I said nonchalantly.

He turned his attention to the screen that was a blank blue color. He tapped another button and sighed. "It's not easy being me," he mumbled toward the screen.

"I hear that," I confirmed.

Joseph spun around in his folding chair. "What?" he asked.

"It's not easy being you," I said.

"You mocking me, again?" he asked.

I ignored the question as I picked up a large piece of banana from the cage floor. "Did you use a strong soap when you washed this cage?" I asked as I examined the chunk of fruit.

"You think you understand me?" he challenged. "I'm fourteen-years-old and smarter than everyone in my class. Heck, I'm on track to graduate from high school two years early. I have colleges calling me every day with scholarships that are contingent on me successfully completing an enormous amount of homework every night. Every person in the school hates me because I mess up the grading curve. I get pushed around by my younger brother and beat up by the jocks in the school. And, on top of all that, I have never kissed a girl."

I stood motionless with half a chunk of banana in my hand as Joseph finished his diatribe. How could this be? A human like me? Well of course there was a human like me. There are so many more of them than us, it stands to reason that there would be at least one or two of them out there. I was almost proud that Joseph caught me.

I had a smart reply for everything Joseph had said up to now. He waited for my response but I was still in shock and could only think of one thing to say. "You've never kissed a girl?" I asked.

"Why don't you just play with that poker game some more," he said disheartened. "I have a lot of homework to do."

"You can't win," I said.

"It's not that bad," he said. "I just need to get started. I'm usually done by dinnertime."

"The poker game," I said. "If you keep playing, you always lose."

"I know," he said.

"Why did you give it to me?" I asked.

"I didn't think you were that smart," he said.

The laptop hummed against the table top. When the screen finally changed from blue, Joseph turned his back to me and began typing. I shoved the last piece of banana into my mouth, picked up the plastic game and sat cross-legged in the corner of my cage. Having nothing better to do, I pressed the "start" button and bet five credits on the next hand. I looked through the wire door at the back of my human intellectual twin and mumbled to myself, "Yeah, me too."

An hour passed and my boredom was at an all-time high. "King of clover, ten of clover, queen of diamond, ace of clover, jack of diamond," I read aloud. I decided to try to get the largest pay-off on every hand. "Throw out the queen and jack and...queen of clover and jack of heart." An ace-high straight was pretty good.

"Joseph," I interrupted to no answer. "Joseph, what'cha doin'?" I asled mimicking Drew who was one of the cooler fairies to ever grace the Touch-and-Go team.

"I'm working," said Joseph.

"Need some help?" I asked.

"Know anything about trigonometry?" he asked sarcastically.

"I know a lot about trigonometry," I said confidently.

"Fairies use trigonometry," he groaned. "Yeah right."

"If I can prove that I know something about trigonometry, will you let me go?" I asked.

He thought for a few seconds then answered, "Probably not."

I thought for a moment then asked, "Will you let me use your laptop?"

"What are you gonna do with a laptop?" he asked.

"What do you do with the laptop?" I asked.

"I do charts and graphs," he began. "I type my papers."

"I don't see any paper," I said.

"It's figurative," he said. "They used to call them papers when people used to write everything on paper but now we just email stuff and turn the files in electronically."

"Oh, right," I said matter-of-factly. I had just established that I was smart and didn't want some terminology to weaken my status. "What else?"

"Research, on the internet," he said.

Research was something I knew about. I had interviewed elders, dug in the soil, dissected plants and sometimes bugs, and read from the writings of the fairies that came before me, but I didn't know anything about an "internet."

"Research on the internet would be cool," I said.

"What are you going to research?" he asked.

"Depends on what's on the internet when I'm doing my research," I said.

"Maybe you could research trigonometry," he laughed.

I took a deep breath then confidently recited, "The imaginary number, written as an italic "i," which represents a value that's not actually real, such as the square root of a negative number, is used to convert the general form of an equation or polynomial into a factored form."

Joseph turned his stunned face around slowly and stared at the cage. I smiled back.

"Do you know how to write English?" he asked.

"I am fluent in speaking and writing many human languages," I said. "If you call the language you speak English, then yes, I write English."

"Help me with my math and I'll hook you up when I'm done with the rest of my homework," he said.

"Any idea when that will be?" I asked patiently.

"Probably after dinner," he said.

I hoped he was a fast eater. I was *really* bored.

CHAPTER TWELVE

Technology

The conversation of a man, a woman, a teenager and a ten-year-old sounded nothing like those I used to have with my parents. Joseph's parents were not as brilliant as he. They did their best to ask questions and understand the challenges he faced in his classwork. But I could hear the silence that I associated with the glazed-over looks of confusion that inevitably covered other's faces as they lost interest in what I was talking about. The conversation was ultimately interrupted by his little brother who was determined to garner his parent's attention.

"Let us know if there's anything we can do to help," said his mother.

"Yeah, Joseph, if there's anything we can do…" added his father.

It was a generous offer but Joseph and I both knew that people like his parents only had two things to offer guys like him and me; love and understanding. I think his parents knew that, too.

The laptop hummed atop the table – its blue screen taunting me like the sky I might never see again. I picked up the poker game and pushed the "Deal" button. King of clover, ten of clover, queen of diamond, ace of clover, jack of diamond. They were identical to the cards I received in the previous hand. "It couldn't do it to me twice in a row," I thought. I again discarded the queen and the jack and hit the draw button. This time I received a queen of clover and a jack of clover. A royal flush; the highest payoff on the machine. The box flashed and buzzed as it added the credits to my bank. Just then, Joseph walked into the room.

"I gotta get that quarter or dollar or whatever you give kids for their teeth," he said. "My brother is serious about getting paid."

"You're gonna have to open the cage for that," I said.

"How about I let you use the computer and you give me a quarter for the tooth?" he bargained.

"I already did half your math homework," I replied. "I earned my time with the laptop."

"Yeah, but I need to get him his money," he said.

"We had a deal," I said. "You gave me your word."

"Yeah, but…"

"A fairy's word is the strongest agreement in any world," I told him.

"Oh, right, you've never gone back on your word?" he asked sarcastically.

I stared him in the eyes and said sternly, "Never."

There was a long silence as he tried to believe that any creature could be so true to their word. My glare and silence conveyed the seriousness of my one-word statement.

"Okay," he said with understanding.

"Okay what...?" I asked.

"How we gonna do this?" he asked. "If I open that door, you're outta here."

"I give you my word as a fairy, as long as you keep your promise, I will not leave."

"And you have to promise not to do any magic like turn me into a frog or a rat or anything," he negotiated.

"I promise. No magic," I agreed.

"You better just give me your wand," he said.

"Why do you need my wand?" I asked. "I gave you my word."

"Then you won't need it, will you?" he answered.

"Never give up your wand" is the first fairy rule you learn after "never fly in the rain." You can tell these rules are important by the absolutes used. "Never" and "always" begin the first ten rules we learn in our colony. But what could he possibly do with my wand? You need fairy wings for it to work and he couldn't know any spells. The worst thing that could happen is

82

he would break it. But it was just a temporary wand. I had planned to get an Oak one when I got promoted to green.

"I have no problems with making this room air tight again and watching your wings fall off like the other night," he warned.

I had no desire to go through that again. I passed the wand through the wire door. It looked tiny in Joseph's hand as he tucked it into a pocket on the side of his backpack then cautiously returned and knelt in front of the cage. He sat anxiously outside the door and stalled. "I'm gonna have to show you how to use it."

"I'm a fast learner," I said as I crawled closer to the door and surveyed the room for places to hide should he not keep his word or something bigger go wrong. For the first time, we were face-to-face. He was really big. His head was half the size of my entire body.

He made a big sigh then pulled his knees up under him and got into a crouch with his arm extended as far away from his body as possible. He reached for the cage door lever and pinched the pins together. Two metal bars pulled away from the top and bottom of the cage. The door swung open violently as Joseph jerked his hand back in fear. His body thudded into the wall as he panicked and backed himself into the corner by the bedroom door.

I looked at the wide-open cage door and then over to Joseph who looked on with fear and suspicion from the corner of the room. He still didn't believe how strong my word was. I tucked my wings against my back so they wouldn't catch on the door frame and took one last look outside the cage. I reached my hand out to hold the cage door open as I walked out, keeping my head and shoulders low to clear the opening. I watched my right foot and then my left foot touch the floor then tilted my head toward Joseph and smiled. I tilted my head to look up at the ceiling that seemed miles above me. I closed my eyes and took a deep breath that helped me straighten my back and stretch my arms. With an equally giant exhale I relaxed my shoulders and dropped my arms to my side, then looked at Joseph and said, "Much better." Joseph slid his body up the wall until he was standing in the corner. "Well?" I asked.

"What?" he asked.

"Hook me up," I said, repeating the phrase he used earlier.

"You have to go back in after I show you how to use it," he said. "You gave me your word."

"You still don't get the power of my word, do you?" I asked. "Are you sure you want your laptop in that cage with the banana pieces and stuff?"

"Just be careful," he said. "Wash your hands before you use it."

"Wash my hands? With what?" I inquired.

"Just don't do anything stupid," he answered.

84

"Just show me how to use it already."

Joseph walked to the table that held the laptop as I fluttered behind him. The screen now had shifting colored lines moving randomly around it. Joseph pushed a plastic orb and the screen changed to the blue glow that I had seen before.

"What did you do?" I asked.

"Moving the mouse makes the screen come back on," he explained.

I jumped up into the air and spun around looking for a rodent. "What mouse?" I asked. "I hate mice."

"It's not a real mouse," he said. "It's this plastic thing. Look."

"I am not touching a mouse," I said.

"Fine" he said, just use the touch pad." Then he showed me how to drag my finger across a rectangle in the front that resulted in an arrow-shaped item gliding across the screen.

That was my introduction to computers. He showed me how to turn it on and off, how to access something called the internet and how to find information on just about anything through something called Bing.

"Do you know how to type?" he asked.

"I don't know what "type" is, but I know how to push down on a button," I answered. "It looks like that's all you have to do."

"That's about it," he said. "It'll do a lot more but all you want is something to read, right?"

"Anything's better than that poker game," I said.

I perched myself on the table in front of the laptop and grinned. My eyes scanned the thing he called a keyboard and I began to memorize the locations of the letters. I dragged my finger across the touch pad until the cursor aligned itself within the search box on the Bing page. I tapped the pad and the cursor flashed inside the box. I considered the plethora of subjects I wanted to learn about. It was almost like making a wish before blowing out the candles on a birthday cake, only I knew I would have more than one wish. Finally I typed the word "teeth" and pressed the "enter" key. The computer made a "bing" sound and twenty-six million, four-hundred-thousand items were found relating to my topic. I would have plenty to read.

Bing!

Joseph read a book while I scanned one of the thousands of pages identified in my search.

"Did you know that kids lose their teeth in two phases?" I asked Joseph rhetorically. "The front teeth fall out between five and eight and the back teeth come out between ten and twelve."

"Wow," was his half-hearted reply.

I searched from teeth to flying to birds to magic. Anything I wanted to learn about was in this little box and all you had to do was type in a question – not even a full question, either – just a couple words. Of course not everything was exactly what you were looking for.

I did a search for Aynil, one of the more famous Traveler Fairies, and the computer asked if I meant "anal." After opening an anal link, I was certain I didn't want anything to do with that. I was surprised at how much stuff I found that I wasn't really looking for. I was really surprised at how much, what I would call "inappropriate material," was readily available. I just assumed some people must need to research that kind of information. I simply chose to ignore it – or at least most of it.

Joseph explained how some companies pay to have their information put at the top of the list of search results. That just gave me another thing to research – advertising. After an hour or so, Joseph yawned a great yawn and said, "Time to go to bed."

"Goodnight," I said as I searched the phrase bedtime.

"That means time to shut down the laptop, too," he said.

"No," I whined, "just a little longer?"

"How long is a little longer?"

"I don't know," I said, "just until I get tired." My teenager negotiating skills returned and I remembered how I used to trick my parents into letting me stay up late. Now that I'm older I realize that I was the one being tricked into extra chores and favors in exchange for the time they knew I would be using anyway. I guess the extra manual labor was worth not dragging a feeling of cheating around with me.

"How long will that be?" he asked.

"I don't know," I answered. "When do you need it back?"

"What are you gonna do, stay up all night?" he asked.

There it was again. One of those perfect set-up questions that begged for my patented response that rolled effortlessly and sarcastically from my lips. It had become habit for me to reply in this manner and before I knew it I rolled my eyes and said, "Wait, wait, I feel a 'duh' coming on."

"Oh you did not just 'duh' me," he said as he abruptly sat up. "Oh, no, no, no. You do not get to "duh" me in my room," he continued as he rose from his bed to retrieve his computer.

"I'm a Tooth Fairy. I work nights," I said.

"Uh, uh," he said as he shooed me away from the screen of data. "You got your time. I kept my word."

"I only got to use it for an hour," I argued.

"I kept my word," he said, "It's time for you to keep yours and get back in your room."

"My room?" I asked.

"It sounds better than kennel," he added.

"Kennel? What am I, a dog," I asked.

"No, but a talking dog might get me more street cred than a Tooth Fairy," he said.

"What's street cred?" I asked. "Let me Bing it."

"It doesn't matter," he said. "Get back in the cage."

"I'll give you a quarter to give to your brother for his tooth," I interjected. Joseph stopped in his tracks.

"You will give me the money to give to my brother if I let you play on the computer?" he asked.

"There's one catch," I added, "I need the tooth."

"The tooth," he repeated.

"I have to have it or I get in big trouble," I said.

Joseph darted toward the bed and ripped one blanket then another and then a sheet off the mattress and shook them. He then ran his hands across the bottom sheet and down between the bed and the wall before getting on his hands and knees and brushing both hands across the floor. He plopped himself on the edge of his bed and looked at me with exasperation. "Do you know where it is?" he asked.

Of course I knew where it was. I knew exactly where it was. The crimson glow behind the desk was a constant reminder of my error in judgment and the possible end of my freedom. The glow wouldn't go away until I had taken possession of the tooth and paid the child who had lost it. But, as much as I wanted the taunting red glow to be gone, I knew I couldn't just make the tooth-for-money exchange for free. I wanted to Bing some more.

"You know," I said cunningly, "I think I saw some information in the computer about finding lost teeth."

"Don't give me that crap," he said disgustedly, "I'm not stupid."

"Look, there's going to be a full moon tonight which means I won't be able to sleep," I recovered, "I just want something to do for tonight and tomorrow when you're gone."

"When do I get the money for my brother?" he bartered.

"When I get the tooth," I answered. "I can't give out money without a tooth."

"I don't know where it is," he said.

"I'll help you find it tomorrow after school," I offered.

Joseph processed the many frustrating thoughts that accompany losing arguments or negotiations. Finally he resolved, "Okay, but you stay in the kennel."

While this may not have been the ideal situation, I had given him my word and he had kept his. He slid the power cord through a slot in the side and placed the laptop on a folded towel toward the back of the dog kennel. I looked up at him, smiled and said "Thank you." It is strange how grateful you become of little favors when you expect to spend the rest of your life in a cage.

CHAPTER FOURTEEN

Words That Hurt

oseph slept loudly. I think that is the nicest way to put it. He snored when he laid on his back and talked in his sleep when he laid on his side or front. He must have used each of those positions six times from the time he went to sleep until the time he was startled awake by the clock alarm. Groggy, as most teenagers are in the morning, he dragged himself from his bed and staggered out the bedroom door. I was reading a page on the computer screen about some book series about a child wizard when a window popped up saying Joseph had a message from JJSMOOTHS95.

I clicked on the window and watched a new page open that welcomed Joseph back to Blastword. It noted that he had twenty-five unread messages and three buddy requests. This page also requested a password. How clandestine. I had not encountered a password request the whole night. This must be a very secret site.

Joseph stumbled back into the room.

"What's your password?" I asked.

He must have still been asleep because he just blurted out, "Cool Cat thirteen, both Cs are capitalized." I punched in the case sensitive password and hit enter.

"You have a message from J-J-Smooths-95," I informed.

"What does it say?" he asked.

"I don't know," I said. "I don't want to get into your personal stuff."

"If you typed in that password you're already into my personal stuff," he said.

The page changed to a full screen with a picture of Joseph in the upper left corner. Under his picture was a list of a bunch of stuff he apparently liked. There were pictures of flying saucers, and musicians and an athlete. I clicked on a button named "photos" and thirty pictures with Joseph filled in the center of the page. There was one of him holding up a fish he had caught and another of him playing basketball against his father. There was one with him and his mother laughing even though they were covered in flour in a kitchen, and one with him and his little brother asleep on the couch. There were photos of him swimming and wrestling with his dad and brother and of climbing trees, but nothing showing his intelligence. Around his room he displayed pictures of his first place science experiments and the day he received the laptop but none of these were on his Blastword page.

"Why don't you have any pictures on this Blastword thing about you being smart?" I asked.

"Because I'm smart," he said. "I'm smart enough to know that no one likes that I'm smart. What does the message say?"

"Bring a whole onion for biology."

"Right," he said to himself. "I almost forgot."

"Looks like you have twenty-five messages in here," I said.

"Yeah, I don't usually read that stuff," he said.

"People are trying to contact you and you just ignore them?" I asked. "That doesn't seem very cordial."

"Cordial?" he questioned. "Read some of the messages."

I clicked on the button and the center screen was filled with other kids' faces and the statements they had sent Joseph. "I heard someone dumped their lunch trash in your backpack. At least you won't have to go dumpster-diving for dinner," I read aloud. "Did someone dump trash in you backpack?" I asked Joseph.

"It wasn't that bad – some guys stuffed some hamburger wrappers in it at lunch one day."

"A lot?" I asked.

"A lot of wrappers?" he clarified. "Twenty-three. The only bad part was they got ketchup on some of my book covers."

I read each of the twenty-five messages left by his so-called "buddies" while he continued dressing. Somewhere out in the sky is a machine that allows people to communicate without paper or ink and, more importantly, without having to be present to see the faces of their victims. I had been insulted and ostracized and gossiped about but the insults had to be delivered face-to-face or would only travel to one or two fairies at a time. Humans could insult you in front of the whole world in only a few seconds with no more effoert than typing a sentence into a laptop. Being a nerd fairy was tough enough but being a nerd human…honestly, I didn't know how Joseph lasted this long.

Joseph pulled a hanger with a neatly pressed blue and white pin-striped seersucker shirt.

"I don't think you want to wear that today," I said.

"Why?" he asked.

"Someone named KARINA1221 says that you wear it all the time and that it makes her want to puke," I read.

Joseph paused and held the shirt and hanger in front of him. I watched his energy field weaken. He became despondent and his arms and face gradually dropped toward the floor as his shoulders sank and he let out a sigh. "It's the best shirt I got," he said.

I knew this feeling. My parents, like I'm sure Joseph's parents, would say it shouldn't bother us. That these kids were stupid and they only hurt other people to make themselves feel better. I'm sure his mother would then promise to take him clothes shopping this weekend which wouldn't help because the new clothes would just become the targets for the next attacks.

I'm sure that most of the time, when Joseph's energy buffer was strong, the insults about his clothes or food or personality wouldn't bother him. But you can only take so many hits before your shields get weak. Joseph didn't wear his best shirt to school that day. I don't think he ever wore it again. It's too bad, it was a nice shirt.

CHAPTER FIFTEEN

Almost Free

$\mathcal{I}$ slowly awoke to a loud pinging sound. My face laid on the touchpad in a pool of spit which stretched into a string of saliva as I groggily raised my head from the keyboard. The computer stopped pinging. I looked at the computer screen to see a page full of Js with some Ks intermixed. I rubbed my hand over the side of my face and felt the indentation of the keys in my skin. I wiped the spit from my mouth then saw the small puddle on the touch pad. I jolted myself awake and quickly wiped the puddle with my shirt tail.

"Oh no," I muttered. "I hope I didn't break it." Thoughts raced through my head. Maybe I broke it and that's why there's a page full of Js. Maybe there's a page full of Js because my face was lying on the "J" key. I knew I should have taken a nap.

I had spent the better part of that day researching what Joseph called Social Medial. In their instant media environment, humans have been trained to react without thinking; to share every thought regardless of how undeveloped it is or who it may hurt. I learned that, in their world of the internet and blogs and tweets, anyone can say anything about anybody with little repercussion. I am most disappointed that much of the disrespectful commentary is posted under the name Anonymous.

How much conviction could a person have in their words if they are not willing to own them? Conversely, how much credence does the unclaimed statement warrant? None. And to take that one step further, what weight should I give a comment posted online or whispered to another person instead of being offered directly to me? A comment delivered in that manner is not done out of love or with the intent of helping to improve me. Those words are meant to do harm or to raise the status of the gossiper. To those who comment out of spite or fear or prejudice or jealousy, I offer condolences and sympathy because you folks have some real issues. But I digress.

Looking for something to change my negative state of mind, I spent the rest of the day (before I fell asleep) surfing the internet and getting as much information on my surroundings as possible. I found out that cats don't like water and some people use squirt guns for training. They spray their cats with water when the animals do something deemed inappropriate. I made a mental note to get some squirt guns. I found out that humans can generate electricity from the sun and they use this electricity to light their homes and power things like the lap top I was using. I made another mental note to get solar panels. I also learned that a dry spring and summer were anticipated for the coming year which meant a high fire danger. I felt bad for the fairies whose colonies are not close to human homes that would be protected by the humans who spray water on fires. In my present incarcerated condition, this information would be a waste, but I assumed that one day I would get to go back to the colony and resume my duties as a Tooth Fairy - if I hadn't already been fired for not returning.

I counted the teeth in my tooth pouch; still nineteen. The twentieth still glowed red behind the bed. I checked my route sheet again. Joseph's address still showed in red on the bottom of the page with the name Andrew. I hoped this meant I was still on the Tooth Fairy roster. I turned my head away from the glowing tooth and back to the laptop screen full of Js and Ks that blocked the back wall of the dog kennel. There was nowhere to look that didn't remind me of my recent mistakes.

I heard sounds of the front door opening and the energetic stampede of Andrew's feet followed by the laboring steps of his mother carrying bags.

"Momma?" asked a small voice. "Why hasn't the Tooth Fairy left me no money?"

"Did you leave your tooth under your pillow?" a female voice replied.

"I don't know," he said.

"Well you have to leave it under your pillow," she said. "Where is your tooth?"

"I don't know," he gave the standard reply.

"Did you take it out of the house?"

"No."

"Where did you have it last?"

"It was in my pocket," he said.

"When was that?" she continued.

"The night it fell out," he said.

"The night it fell out of your mouth?" she clarified.

"Yeah," he answered.

"That was two nights ago," she said. "Weren't you wrestling with Joseph that night?"

"I don't know," he said.

"Heavens, boy, when aren't you wrestling with your brother," she said. "I think you should go look in Joseph's room."

"Okay," he said enthusiastically.

I heard the sound of little feet running toward the door and stopping. I watched the doorknob twist followed by a simultaneous thud and grunt. The door did not open. I closed the lid to the laptop so the glow of the screen would not attract attention. Again I heard a thud and a grunt with no door movement.

"Momma, it's stuck," said the small voice.

"I'm coming," she said which was followed by a combination of quick thuds and grumbles which stopped outside the door. "He can't lock this can he?" she asked. Then the doorknob twisted again followed by a louder grunt and larger thud and the door flew open. "There," she said. "Don't move anything and don't play with anything; your brother is the only one in this family who keeps a neat room." Then she left the little boy standing in the doorway. I tucked my wings behind me and sat perfectly still hoping he would find his tooth and leave. His head and eyes turned back and forth as different items caught his attention.

He was in here two nights ago but things in Joseph's room changed every day as the older brother found new challenges. The little boy strolled into the room and toward the bed where he and Joseph played.

His older brother would pick him up and toss him onto the stack of mattresses and then pounce on him as if he were a professional wrestler. Andrew didn't know how Joseph never hurt him with this move. Maybe he was just a lot stronger than Joseph and could take the beating. In actuality, Joseph would strategically place his arm and forearm to hold his body weight off his little brother and pretend to slam himself upon the small boy's chest. It was one of these moves that bounced the tooth from the Andrew's pocket and under Joseph's pillow.

The little man dove onto the bed and began rummaging through the sheet and blankets. It wasn't long before he became distracted and stopped searching for the tooth. Instead he became an explorer in a cave. He made animal sounds and described dangerous caverns as he squirmed under the blanket. If I played things right, this kid was my way out.

"I know where your tooth is," I said coyly.

"What?" came the reply as the once rustling cave of sheets and blankets stood motionless.

"I know where your tooth is," I said again.

There was loud grunting and rustling and kicking and thrashing until the boy emerged from under the blankets and knelt on the bed. "Who said that?" he asked as he scanned the room. "Booker, are you in here. You better not be in here or my dad is gonna hurt you hard."

"I'm in the cage," I said.

The boy's eyes darted toward the kennel. He cautiously stepped from the bed and walked toward the cage door noting that the power cord for the laptop snaked through the side panel. He knelt beside the front gate and looked in. "Where did you get that?" he asked pointing toward the laptop. "Who are you?"

"I am Darvin and your brother let me use his computer," I replied pleasantly.

"My brother doesn't let nobody use his computer."

"Well, I traded him my wand," I said.

"What do you need a wand for?" he asked.

"Can you keep a secret?" I whispered.

His eyes grew large and a giant smile spread across his face as he said "Yes."

"Are you sure?" I asked. "This is a really big secret. You have to promise not to tell anyone, ever."

"I promise I won't tell anyone," he swore.

"Okay," I said as I scanned his face one more time to see if I was being played. I continued, "I know where your tooth is because..." I began.

"Where," he interrupted. "Did you take it?"

"No," I said calmly, "I came here to get it from under your pillow and leave you a quarter. I am the Tooth Fairy."

"No way," he shouted. "I'm telling my mom." And he stood up to leave.

"You promised," I whispered sternly.

"So, you're lying," he replied.

"Oh no," I gasped, "You called a Tooth Fairy a liar. Do you know what Tooth Fairies do to kids who call them liars?"

He stopped and turned around. "What?" he asked.

"I can't tell you," I answered.

"Why?" he asked.

"Because it's a secret and it's obvious that you can't keep a secret," I began. "You were going straight to your mom when I said I was the Tooth Fairy. That means you didn't keep your promise either. I guess you're going to have to find out the hard way what happens to kids who call us liars and don't keep promises."

"I wasn't really going to tell her," he lied.

"Sure, you were just joking," I said. "I guess we'll see whose laughing when a whole bunch of fairies show up in your bedroom while you're sleeping and… I don't even want to think about it."

"Think about what?" he asked nervously. "What are they going to do?"

"I'm really not supposed to tell you but I'll make you a deal," I bargained. "Let me out of the cage and I'll make sure it doesn't happen to you."

"You'll make sure what doesn't happen to me?"

"The thing I can't tell you," I answered.

"How do I know if it's a bad thing if you don't tell me what it is?" he asked.

"Trust me, it's bad," I answered.

"Can you give me a hint?"

I paused to formulate an appropriate yet vague response and said, "Let me ask you a question. Do you like eating solid food?"

"What's solid food?" the boy asked to my surprise. I began to wonder if Joseph was adopted. I worked to contain my emotions while I tried a different approach.

"Okay, let's forget the whole not-keeping-your-word thing," I countered. "How about, you let me out,

I show you where your tooth is, and trade you money for your tooth?"

"Isn't that what the Tooth Fairy does?" he replied.

"I AM THE TOOTH FAIRY!" I shouted. The outburst set the boy aback so I repeated in a more calm and controlled tone, "I am the Tooth Fairy."

"Shouldn't you have wings?"

"Let me out and I'll show them to you," I said.

The boy sat there wondering what to do next. His mind raced between what he wanted and how mad his brother would get if he came home and his Tooth Fairy was out of the cage. His small hands reached toward the cage, he grabbed the mesh door and pulled but nothing happened. He grabbed it tighter and shook but that only caused me and the laptop to be bounced around inside. The sound of the apartment door opening and slamming shut was followed by Joseph's voice calling out to his brother.

"Andrew?"

"I don't know how to open it," said Andrew.

"Just squeeze the brackets together," I said.

"Andrew, where are you?" called Joseph again. The sound of footsteps got louder. All I needed was half a second more and I would be free. Then all I had to do was make sure the room had fresh air so I didn't lose my wings. Once I got my wand back, I could Drape-and-Shoot my way out of here. Andrew had both of his hands squeezing on the brackets. I watched as each post drew further away from the edge. My legs were primed to vault me out the door once the slightest opening was revealed. The footsteps got louder with the grunting sounds of the little boy who was opening the door to my freedom.

"Andrew, get away from there," yelled Joseph from the doorway.

The little boy jumped up and ran to the side of the bed where he stood nervously at attention with his hands behind his back. Joseph tossed his backpack on the ground and rushed to the cage to ensure it was still locked. I only saw his face for a moment but something was different.

"What are you doing in here?" scolded Joseph.

"Mom said I could look for my tooth," cried Andrew.

"Well it isn't in here," said Joseph.

"He said it is," said Andrew as he pointed to the cage. "He said he would help me find it and give me a quarter if I let him out."

"Oh yeah," said Joseph. "Why would you believe him?"

"Cause he's the Tooth Fairy," said Andrew.

"I'll find your tooth," Joseph said with a scowel.

"Is he the Tooth Fairy?" asked Andrew.

"Does he look like a Tooth Fairy?" Joseph replied. "He doesn't even have wings."

"He said the cage is too small," said Andrew. Joseph didn't reply. "If he's not a Tooth Fairy, what is he?"

"I don't know," said Joseph. "Maybe he's an elf or a troll."

"Okay, buddy," I blurted out. "Now you've gone too far. A troll?! It's bad enough being compared to a grounded being like an elf but to go subterranean is just plain rude."

"I'll deal with you in a minute," replied Joseph.

"No, you'll deal with me now," I said sternly.

"Andrew, you better leave," said Joseph.

"Yeah, little man, this isn't going to be pretty," I added.

Joseph led Andrew out the door then closed and locked it behind him. That's when the fireworks started.

"Who do you think you are getting my little brother to let you out," shouted Joseph.

"I'm the fairy in the cage, you idiot!" I shouted back. "What would you do if you had my wings?"

"What's that supposed to mean?"

"Oh, right, I think humans say something like 'if you were in my shoes,' or something that doesn't have to do with flying and being free!" I yelled.

"I never said I wasn't going to let you go," he said.

"You never said you would either, did you?" I retorted. "There's no room in here to stretch my legs or my wings, you barely feed me – which is good because one of these days I'm going have to purge my system and that will definitely not be pretty. I love bananas but they really bind me up inside. But, like my father always said, 'all things must pass.'"

"That's just gross," he said.

"That is the destiny of this cage if you don't let me go," I said.

"You want to go? Fine!" Joseph stormed over and knelt in front of the cage. It was then that I saw what was different. His left eye was swollen and the area around it had tints of red and blue that were not as noticeable from a distance because of his dark skin. "You've been nothin' but trouble since I caught you. For a minute I thought I might get some cred with the kids at school but no one believes in fairies." Joseph unlatched the cage door and stood up, leaving it ajar. It gradually swung open as he stormed back to his make-shift desk. "I can't believe I was so stupid."

I stepped from the cage and dusted myself off. I unfolded my wings and shook them loose. While Joseph unpacked his backpack, I fluttered over to the red glow behind his bed and picked Andrew's tooth from the floor. Then I flew to the table where Joseph stood in tears. I held the tooth out to him and asked, "Who hit you?"

CHAPTER SIXTEEN

Pain and Suffering

Joseph got upset and turned away from me. He was ashamed and embarrassed that he would let someone do this to him. Normally I wouldn't assume how a person felt but this was no assumption on my part; I knew what he was feeling. I had felt it before when the same things happened to me.

"Who did this to you?" I asked.

"Nobody," he replied.

"Don't think I don't know what's going on here," I insisted. "I know what black eyes look like and where they come from."

Joseph sighed. "If I had my choice, I would be home schooled, but my mom says regular schools are better and that the social interaction is important. She doesn't have to deal with the kids I have to. There's this guy who picks on me. I don't know why. I've never done anything to hurt anyone. I don't make fun of people, like you do."

"Like me?" I asked surprised.

"Wait, wait, I feel a 'duh' coming on?"

"Oh, right," I acknowledged.

"I just try to do my best and move on. But they seem to get some thrill out of calling me names and bumping me in the hall. I try to get to school early so I see them as little as possible. But there's this one guy, Ricky Stevens, who never seems to leave the place. He's sitting in the hall when I get there and hanging around outside 'til everybody leaves. And the thing is, he doesn't even notice me unless there are other kids around.

"Today, Ricky shows up with a swollen face and missing a tooth after a baseball accident yesterday. He said he lost the ball in the sun. I thought it was peculiar because he isn't on the baseball team so I asked him who he was playing with. He said that it was some guys I didn't know and told me to shut up about it. Well, me knowing you now, I suggested he put the tooth under his pillow so he could at least get some money. I guess he thought I was mocking him. So I showed him your wand, thinking that it would give my story more credibility. He grabbed it and tried to snap it in half but couldn't. What are those things made of?"

"Treated maple," I answered as I cringed at the thought of my wand being snapped in two. Without it, I couldn't Drape-and-Shoot which means I would be limited to human access points to get out of this house.

"Don't worry," said Joseph, "I grabbed it from his hands before he could do any damage. That made him more angry and he reacted with the same violence he did when anyone took something from him. I told everyone I hit a bedpost wrestling with Andrew."

Oh, man, was I mad. I was so angry that I couldn't fly straight. I wanted to teach this Ricky Stevens a lesson and I knew how to do it.

"Did he keep the tooth?" I asked.

"What?" said Joseph.

"The tooth he was missing, did he still have it?"

"Yeah, he was showing it to everyone like it was a trophy or something," he answered.

"Do you want him to stop picking on you?" I asked.

Joseph rolled his eyes, held up his index finger signaling me to wait, then said with great sarcasm, "Wait, wait, I feel a 'duh' coming on."

The irony of my own catch phrase coming back didn't faze me. I was focused. "I can get him for you," I said. "As long as he has a free tooth in the house, I can get to him. But I need my wand."

"Oh no," Joseph started. "No, no, no, no, no. I give you this wand and you're gone. I'm not letting you go that easily."

"I am offering you my services for free as long as you give me back my freedom," I argued.

111

"I don't know about that," he said.

"You said you weren't going to keep me forever," I argued.

"What are you going to do to him?" he asked.

"We Tooth Fairies reserve the right to penalize anyone we feel has not treated others with respect. Since we deal only in money and teeth, the penalties tend to revolve around tooth extraction. Sometimes the term becomes plural."

"How plural?" he asked.

"Very plural. Completely and totally plural, if you understand," I answered. "I don't think you will see this boy in school for a while."

"How long is 'a while'?"

"How long do dentures take these days?"

Joseph pondered the proposed penalty for a minute. "What if you don't do it? I will have let you go free for nothing."

"I give you my word," I began, "I will either do what I have just vaguely described or I will return to your home and allow you to put me back in the cage until you choose to release me."

Joseph again pondered the options then walked quickly to his backpack and removed my wand. "Your word." He confirmed.

"My word," I answered.

He reached the wand out toward me. "Do you

want me to find his address?" he asked.

I swooped down and grasped the polished maple stick from his hand. "I don't need it," I said confidently, "I find loose teeth for a living." Then I did the Drape-and-Shoot, darted through the pane of glass and was on my way.

CHAPTER SEVENTEEN

Revenge

I flew toward the human school because Joseph said that this Stevens guy lived on the other side of town. I had no real idea what he looked like other than he was bigger than Joseph and was missing a tooth which he had in his pocket. I would look for the white glow of the tooth. All teeth glow white until they are assigned to a Tooth Fairy for retrieval. If I found it before it was assigned by the Tooth Fairy Manager, I could make a claim on the tooth which would be noted in the TFM's log. This would no doubt generate some commotion around the colony considering I had been missing for two days. I would deal with that later.

I weaved between tree branches and behind larger structures trying to stay hidden. I reached the school without seeing a boy or a white glow and continued up Elm Street as Joseph had instructed. Elm was one of those streets in one of those neighborhoods where all the trees and all of the houses on the street are the same.

The smaller, red brick homes had front porches that nobody used and nice, green lawns that were maintained by the homeowners. When you've been around as many houses as I have, you can tell when someone has a gardener.

I was glad it was Elm Street instead of Aspen or Pine. The streets named after trees were lined with those trees and Aspens and Pines are hard to fly through and offered very little cover. Elms are large trees with big leaves that were great for hiding and resting in during the day. I was about to dart into an especially old Elm when I saw the white glow of a lost tooth and what must have been Ricky Stevens trudging home under the weight of a tattered backpack and whatever other emotional baggage he was carrying.

He was a tall kid, about twenty-four leaves when he stood up straight which he didn't do very often. He carried a stick that he must have snapped off a tree because it still had autumn leaves on the end which he tried to dislodge by slapping the stick against fence posts and tree trunks along the way. The branch had three golden leaves left which he worked diligently to detach when he reached the last house on the block. After five violent swings at the trunk of the large elm in the front yard, he gave up on the last leaf and tossed the stick on the ground. He trudged around to the side of the house to see the garage door open and two older vintage cars parked in the driveway. Music and loud talking poured out the door. Ricky hesitated and almost jealously looked at the simple and bland neighboring houses.

Ricky's tooth glowed brightly as he walked quickly through the shadow of the north side of the house. I had allowed myself to get caught up in the chase and almost forgot to place my claim on the tooth.

I drew my wand and said the incantation "mycuspid" and the tooth's glow changed to my familiar red color just before Ricky entered the side door of the house. I was now officially invited in.

Nightfall was still hours away. Ricky's reaction to the cars in the driveway peaked my curiosity so I flew to the side of the street opposite the open garage door and hid in the maple tree beside the sidewalk. I could see three men sitting and talking and drinking beer at a brisk pace. Fairies have been around long enough to know that human consumption of large amounts of alcohol is not good.

Normally I would wait until dark to enter a house but I wanted to get a feel for the place and find hiding spots should I need them. If Ricky's father was going to be drunk, I needed to be able to stay covered. Sober humans see fairies all the time but, because they don't believe in us, they typically discard what they saw as an illusion. We are usually gone by the time they decide to look back. But drunken humans tend not to doubt their first impressions and will follow and chase us. The key to handling drunk people is to not be seen in the first place.

I fluttered down beside an open bedroom window and, making sure everything was clear, did the Drape-and-Shoot. I was in. I listened for sounds that would tell me if someone was coming but only heard cabinet doors opening and closing in the kitchen. I took a moment to familiarize myself with the surroundings.

The bedroom was small and messy. The two-human bed was unmade after a violent night's sleep and there were dirty clothes on the floor. The top of the dresser was cluttered with loose change, business cards and those rubber wrist bands that were popular in the early two-thousands. "I'll be right back," bellowed a voice followed by the sound of a light door squeaking open and slamming shut. The following conversation ensued.

"Thank you, don't mind if I do," said Ricky's father.

"Hey, that's my sandwich," shouted Ricky.

"I haven't had lunch today," said his dad.

"Me either," shouted Ricky.

"Whose fault is that? Get your butt out of bed earlier and you'll have time to make your lunch." There was no reply. "Just make another one," instructed the father.

"There's no more bread," said Ricky.

"Guess you need to go to the store, then," was his father's snide reply. "While you're there, get one of those frozen pizzas for everyone. There's money on the dresser."

"I'm not going to the grocery store," said Ricky.

"Listen, you piece of crap, I've been working all day and I have company over. Go to the damn store and get a pizza or, so help me, I'll knock out another tooth. Do you get me?"

There was a pause then Ricky said, "How am I supposed to get there?"

"I don't give a rat's ass. Walk. Take your damn bike," said his dad.

Feet stomped in my direction and I took cover in the closet. Ricky stormed into the bedroom wiping tears from his face. He rummaged through the pile of stuff on the dresser until he gathered enough money and stormed out of the room. I listened as the footsteps got further away and the screen door slammed. The house was quiet except for the sounds of the music and voices that crept in from the garage. This was not what I expected.

A Change of Plans

The house was empty for the thirty minutes it took Ricky to go to the store and back. I used the time to explore the rooms and look for hiding places. I found a place in the living room behind the couch and one in each of the three small bedrooms – one of which was more like an office. The kitchen offered no places to hide but I could comfortably stay out of reach atop the cabinets. I could go to the basement as a last resort. The problem with basements is that they were usually air tight.

The house was pretty well maintained, other than the room I chose as access to the house. Ricky's room was easy to identify. It was the one with the single human bed and posters on the walls of beautiful women holding tools. I made a note to myself to get pictures of tammies holding wands. The room wasn't clean but it was uncluttered. The difference between clean and uncluttered can be measured by the amount of dust on the top of the dresser and under the bed. This room needed dusting.

I perched myself under the bed in Ricky's room and waited for his return. I was starting to lose my disdain for the poor kid and half hoped that he would kick a dog or hurt another defenseless being so I could justify pulling all his teeth, as I had promised. But when Ricky returned, he coldly went about the business of placing a frozen pizza in the oven and putting the rest of the grocery items away. Sounds of dishes being washed and put away, as well as other cleaning sounds, lasted another half-hour until a beeping sound was interrupted and then I heard sounds of a pan or tray being tossed onto a counter.

A minute later Ricky trod into his bedroom with his backpack and a paper plate with two slices of pizza and collapsed into a small chair at a desk. He slid a math book and a pad of paper onto the desk and sighed. He tried to take a big bite from the pizza slice but there was a large gap in his bite from his missing tooth and he did not completely sever the crust or the cheese. As he pulled his bite away from the whole, the cheese slid off the remaining crust and pulled the toppings and sauce onto his shirt.

"Dang it!" he yelled as he slammed the plate on the desk then ripped the pizza toppings from his shirt and slammed them back onto the empty crust. He quickly pulled off his shirt. The violent move sent his tooth flying out of his pocket and under the bed where I was hiding. He ran to the kitchen and desperately tried to rinse the red sauce out of his shirt. That's when his dad came inside.

"Where's the pizza?" he asked gruffly.

"On the stove," said Ricky equally gruffly.

"What did you do, drop a piece on your shirt?" his dad said as he strolled to the stove and grabbed the pan with the remaining slices. "How many pieces did you take?"

"I took a quarter of it," said Ricky.

"What makes you think you need a quarter of a pizza?"

"I rode to the store and got the thing and I made it," argued Ricky.

"Did you pay for it?" asked his dad.

"What?"

"Hell no, you didn't pay for it. I paid for it. I'll decide who gets how much."

"Why can't I have as much as you guys?"

"Cause they're company," he said.

"But I live here. I keep the place clean. I mow the lawn. I do the laundry. All they do is sit in the garage and drink beer."

"They're company," said his dad coldly. "I hope you bought another one while you were there."

"I only bought the one," said Ricky.

"Then it looks like you better go get another one," said his dad with a drunken grin.

"I can't," said Ricky, "I have homework."

"Homework?!" shouted his dad.

"Math and English," Ricky shouted back. "I probably would've been done with half of it if I didn't have to get that stupid pizza."

Ricky's dad pinched Ricky's trapezius muscle making Ricky grimace in pain. "Don't you ever raise your voice to me, you hear?" Ricky jerked is body away from his father. "You think you're smart?" said his dad. "Well I'm pretty smart too. I'm smart enough to know that homework never rebuilt no carburetors and fixin' carburetors is what pays for this house. If you want to keep stayin' here, you better cool it with your attitude."

His dad left the kitchen with the rest of the pizza. Ricky, frustrated, slammed the shirt into the sink and stormed back to his bedroom. He threw himself on the bed so hard that I thought the mattress would crush me under the box. He pounded on the mattress then punched his pillow as he cursed his father and his father's friends and wondered why his mother didn't take him with her when she left. And when the weight of everything he was feeling became too much, he pushed his face into his tenderized pillow and cried.

Ricky didn't get his homework done, again. He

tried. As is sometimes the case, he became stronger after crying out the pain and frustration of the day. He took this new energy and focused on his math homework which, as it turned out, he was pretty good at. But the energy surge wasn't enough to keep him awake long enough to finish his reading for English and he fell asleep with the book open on his chest. My opportunity had arrived.

I crouched under the bed pondering what I had just witnessed. I wished I had taken more time to research bullies when I had access to Joseph's laptop. I doubt I would have made the promise I made if I had known this was a possibility. I crawled across the floor and retrieved the glowing tooth from the corner then crept out from under the bed.

Two quick beats of my wings put me atop the mattress where I stared at this very large child who was probably a good kid but was stuck in a bad situation. I remembered back not so long ago when I had the opportunity to really hurt another bully and didn't. I would not start now.

I held the tooth in my outstretched hand and waved my wand over it using a sterilization spell with a livening incantation. Two more beats of my wings placed me beside his head. I tilted his head away from me to expose the side that the tooth had come from, pushed his lip up to expose the hole, and shoved the tooth back into place. A quick wave of my wand to remind the gums to take it back and I was done. Then I figured, since I already had my hand in his mouth, I might as well go ahead and straighten the teeth and make them a little whiter.

I stepped back to admire my work and wondered what Ricky's reaction would be in the morning when he saw his new mouth. I remembered the excitement of the younger kids who I had left money for, but did not know what to expect from a teenager.

I heard the sound of the screen door opening and the muffled goodbyes of Ricky's father to his friends. It was time to go. And, whether I liked it or not, I would be returning to Joseph and to the cage.

CHAPTER NINETEEN

Promise Keeping

$\mathcal{M}$y exit was flawless and swift – just like the hundreds of times I had done it before my encounter with Joseph. I popped out of Ricky's window and into the middle of a cluster of Tooth Fairies.

"Darvin!" cried my mother as she threw her arms around me. Everyone else, my father, Gaylord, Spandlin, Derf, Columbine, the Tooth Fairy Manager and a couple other fairies that I didn't expect, Clare and Alpho, fluttered in silence until my mother loosened her hug, grabbed me by the shoulders and shouted, "Where have you been!"

Almost everyone talked at the same time so I only caught bits and pieces of what they said. My father expressed the importance of trying to communicate even if you are caught. Gaylord, Spandlin and Derf told varying stories of how they had been looking for me for the past two days and even missed school which Derf made a point of letting me know how that might negatively affect his grade. The Tooth Fairy Manager informed me that I would need to be debriefed and there would be some paperwork to fill out. Columbine just fluttered there tapping her wand in her hand and looking at me. Things started to get loud.

"Do you really want to do this right here outside a human's window?" I shouted. The crowd hushed.

"I saw a cottonwood twenty-one wing beats to the south," said Columbine. "Follow me."

We followed Columbine to the large cottonwood which was exactly twenty-one wing beats to the south.

The group clustered near the top of the large tree where the bare branches and remaining colored leaves could hide us from human view. This is where I shared my story of the brilliant human boy and the cage I was in for the past two days. Finally I said, "And that is why I have to go back." There was silence as I looked at the faces of my family, friends and co-workers.

"No, you can't go back there," demanded my Mom. "He doesn't have to go back, does he?" she asked the Tooth Fairy Manager.

"He was under duress," said Spandlin.

"Yeah, any one of us would have said anything to get out of that situation," added Gaylord.

"He gave his word," said the Tooth Fairy Manager solemnly. "We all know the penalty for not keeping your word."

"It can't be as bad as living in a cage and barely eating," said my Mom.

"Trust is a difficult thing to re-establish," said the Tooth Fairy Manager. "It can take years to clear your name. He must complete "The Tasks of Honesty." He will be grounded until he has completed all twelve."

"No one's ever succeeded," whispered Alpho to Clare.

"What?" asked my mom.

"No one's ever succeeded," I blurted out. "Most get eaten by cats or knocked out of a tree. With no wings and no magic, they have no way to protect themselves.

"Look, Mom, I gave him my word," I said.

"But he's just a human," she cried.

"That may work to Darvin's advantage," said my dad. "There is always a chance the human will let him go."

"Humans are a pretty forgiving species," said Derf.

"There are lots of stories about humans being kind to fairies," added Gaylord.

"You know that's true," my Dad reminded my mom. "Your own father tells the story of the time he was trapped in a human's garage. He still visits that man on occasion."

"It's getting late," I said. "I have to go. Being tardy is almost as bad as being absent, if I've learned correctly." Columbine and the Tooth Fairy Manager both nodded. "I only promised to return," I reminded them.

"I didn't say I wouldn't try to escape."

I hugged my parents then fluttered backward off the branch. I offered one last look and smile to each of my friends then, with one giant thrust of my wings, I darted toward the stars.

I arrived at Joseph's window only minutes before the time I was due to return. I wasn't certain how he would react to the news that I had fixed Ricky's tooth instead of collecting the rest of them. From the two days I spent with him, I don't think he truly would have enjoyed seeing another person in that much pain but brilliant people come in all shapes and sizes. Some become the likes of Albert Einstein and Gandhi while others become the Unibomber and Osama Bin Laden. I took one last look at the stars and hoped that Joseph might at least point the cage door toward the window so I could reminisce about the times I used to fly just outside the panes of glass. I took my wand into my right hand and Drape-and-Shooted myself into the room.

Joseph sat at the desk cleaning my spit off the touchpad. I hovered in front of him as he focused his attention on the keys and screen.

"I didn't expect you back," he said.

"I didn't either," I said.

"So you didn't keep your word," he said.

"Yes, I did," I answered. "I came back, just as I promised."

"You promised to take all his teeth out," he argued. "You promised you would make him pay for what he did to me; for everything he did to me. You gave me your word."

"Things are not as black and white as I thought," I answered. "I promised that I would come back if I didn't follow through. Here I am."

"Great!" he said sarcastically. "What am I gonna do with a Tooth Fairy? I hope you ate while you were out because we don't have any more bananas."

"If you were me, I think you would have done the same thing," I said.

"If I were you? If I were you?" he began. "If I were you I would fly away from this place and hide in the trees and live without all these expectations piled upon me. If I were you I could wave a wand and zip people's mouths closed or make their teeth crumble when they chewed if they were mean to me. If I were you, I wouldn't have to take crap from anyone. I could be myself without being picked on. I could finally live in peace."

"Is that how you think my life is?" I asked. "Do you think I live a carefree life with no worries or concerns? I graduated from high school early, just like you. I blew up the grading scale for every class I took, just like you. And I got punched and pushed and used by people, just like you. 'If I were you?' Joseph, I am you. Our lives aren't just similar, they're identical. We live in parallel universes. I couldn't be more like you unless I got demoted and got a really good tan." I took a few deep breaths and we both calmed down before I continued. "You know I was afraid to fly until I was thirteen? Being really smart has its down side, too."

"Who's ever heard of a fairy afraid to fly?" he said.

"Look at the size of these things," I said commenting on my wings. "Do these really look like they'll carry my weight?"

"They do kind of look like bee wings," he said.

"A walking fairy is about the biggest nerd or freak you're going to find," I said.

"I'm guessing you were a pretty easy target," he said.

"Black eyes show up better on white faces," I said. "My school life was very difficult, too. Fortunately, I had very smart and supportive parents."

Joseph looked toward the door where we heard the voices of his mom and dad talking in the kitchen. "They are supportive," he said.

"That alone means they're smart," I said.

There was a silence as Joseph considered the many good things in his life then he asked, "So what happened at Ricky's house?"

I sat on the edge of the table and shared the story of my afternoon and evening and about the boy whose life would be changed by a frozen pizza. I looked into Joseph's eyes and tried to connect with his eem so as to not mislead him with false emotion. I wanted him to feel exactly what I felt. Finally I said, "And that is why I came back," and waited patiently for his response – one that I hoped and expected would confirm my choice of actions.

"You left a note that said I told you to fix his tooth?" he asked.

"I hoped it might get you some street cred," I answered.

"I guess we'll find out," he said.

"You can tell him that I said he should floss more."

"May as well go all in," Joseph chuckled.

"Okay," I sighed, "I'm glad we got that over with. I'm ready to go back in the cage." I reached down and grabbed the poker game off the table top. "Mind if I take this with me?" I asked. "It will be some entertainment since I doubt you'll let me use the computer."

"You can use the computer whenever you want – as long as I don't need it," he said. "But you have to promise to keep your slobber off it."

"I apologize," I said.

"I also think you need to get back to work," he added. "I hear they're running short on Tooth Fairies."

"You're letting me go?" I asked.

"After you take care of my brother," he confirmed.

I remembered the story about my mom's dad and the human he still visited. Had I found a human of my own?

"Thank you," I said.

I handed him the poker game, strapped my coin changer around my waste, and confirmed it was working by pressing the lever which dispensed one coin. I turned back toward Joseph and showed him the quarter.

He smiled at me, and I at him, then I darted into the next room where Andrew's head rested on a pillow that glowed red from the tooth underneath.

CHAPTER TWENTY

In Conclusion

"The answers you seek are in the color of the moon."
I had a lot of time to consider that statement when Joseph let me go. I spent hours looking at the orb in the sky searching for the obvious answer that I just knew I had overlooked. It wasn't until I gave up trying and saw the moon for what it was – a bunch of shades of gray – that I understood.

Life is not black or white. In life, right and wrong, good and bad, funny and not funny, will always be tempered by our own experiences. That is why it is best to be slow to judge or react to the actions of others – unless, of course, their actions are causing you physical harm. In that case, I recommend a front, two-knuckle punch to the kisser. But only in self-defense.

I returned to Joseph's house regularly to work on the laptop. My tooth gathering numbers dropped as I chose to spend time correcting misinformation about fairies from assorted website pages instead of trading money for teeth. I thought developing a better understanding between humans and fairies would render greater future benefits. In exchange for computer time, I served as a sounding board for Joseph during some of his more trying times and taught him human versions of my Asian self-defense techniques. Fortunately, he never needed to use them. Joseph and I remain friends to this day.

It turned out that the Tooth Fairy job was temporary. The next two graduating classes had a large number of talented flyers who actually wanted the job. I was disappointed that I missed the fairly obvious data and wasn't more prepared when I was called to participate in the post-graduation ceremony. This time the Great Cottonwood said, "To be in the present, you must look to the future." This time I exited more graciously with a pair of temporary wings.

I moved to Add Ed where I learned that everyone is insecure about something and that everyone knows that there is something in this world that they are very good at. It is when we allow our insecurities and the insecurities of others to diminish our confidence in our unique talents that we do the most damage to ourselves and the world we were sent to improve. That is why I have grown more patient with those less adept at learning and have found myself trying to help others more and criticize them less.

But there are times when the answer to a question is ridiculously obvious and the person's inability to recognize this is not due to ignorance or stupidity but, instead, the result of pure laziness. On these rare occasions, I smile and playfully say, "Wait, wait, I feel a 'duh' coming on."

FAIRY TERMS

AD ED
Short for Additional Education. The fairy version of college.

BEING PULLED
The painful sensation a Traveler Fairy experiences in their shin when it is time for him/her to move on to their next destination. Introduced in *The Tale of Aynil the Traveler*.

DRAGGING
when a Traveler Fairy stays in a location even though they are being pulled toward a new destination. Introduced in *The Tale of Aynil the Traveler*.

DRAPE-AND-SHOOT
the spell used to get Tooth Fairies in and out of houses.

EEM
The mystical energy fairies have that allows them to connect emotionally and spiritually with another fairy. Used primarily to share personal experiences with others. Introduced in *The Tale of Rebecca the Chased*.

EEMING
When two or more fairies are connecting through their eems.

LEAF
A measurement of length equaling three inches or 76 millimeters

PINCHING PENNIES
A general term for taking human money from Leprechaun traps. The money does not have to be pennies.

STONE
A measurement of weight equaling 8 ounces or 227 grams.

TAMMY
A pretty girl fairy.

TOUCH-AND-GO
A flying game played by fairies that is similar to Hide-and-Seek. Introduced in *The Tale of Rebecca the Chased*.

Paul Vincent Rodriguez was raised in the small town of Alma, Michigan. He spent a lot of time in the woods of the northern Lower Peninsula where nature had not yet been disturbed and where magical creatures prevail. It wasn't until he had children that he found that magic is everywhere—even in cities. It is his hope that someday, everyone will be able to see the magic too.

Coming Soon

TALES OF FAIRIES

The Tale of

Flaylen

THE Fallen

TALES OF FAIRIES

The Tale of

Rhine

THE Warrior

www.ingramcontent.com/pod-product-compliance
Lightning Source LLC
Chambersburg PA
CBHW021110130626
46554CB00002B/615

* 9 7 8 0 9 8 4 3 2 8 1 8 5 *